Waiting for Damon . . .

I pounced on the phone and hit the talk button before the first ring had even ended.

"Hello?" My heart was in my throat, and I was gripping the phone so hard it almost popped out of my hand.

"Hey, Jess," Damon's voice resonated through the speaker.

"Hey!" I said, sitting up straight.

"Listen, can I speak to Elizabeth?" Damon said.

At least that was what I thought he said.

"What?" I asked.

"Is Elizabeth around?" he asked, this time sounding tired and annoyed.

Part of me wanted to just yell at him—ask him who he thought he was, calling here and asking for my sister instead of me after I'd been wondering where he was all afternoon. But I was too angry and confused to put my thoughts into any kind of coherent order. Instead I just thrust the phone toward my sister without saying good-bye. Then I got up and walked out of the room. There was no way I was going to stick around and listen to my sullen, distant boyfriend joke around with my sister.

Don't miss any of the books in SWEET VALLEY JUNIOR HIGH, an exciting series from Bantam Books!

SWEET VALLEY jr. high

She Loves Me ... Not

Written by
Jamie Suzanne

Created by
FRANCINE PASCAL

BANTAM BOOKS
NEW YORK • TORONTO • LONDON • SYDNEY • AUCKLAND

RL 4, 008–012

SHE LOVES ME . . . NOT
A Bantam Book / July 2000

Sweet Valley Junior High is a trademark of Francine Pascal.
Conceived by Francine Pascal.
Cover photography by Michael Segal.

Produced by 17th Street Productions,
an Alloy Online, Inc. company.
33 West 17th Street
New York, NY 10011.

ISBN: 0-553-48721-3

Visit us on the Web! www.randomhouse.com/kids

Published simultaneously in the United States and Canada

Bantam Books is an imprint of Random House Children's Books, a
division of Random House, Inc. BANTAM BOOKS and the rooster
colophon are registered trademarks of Random House, Inc. Bantam Books,
1540 Broadway, New York, New York 10036.

PRINTED IN THE UNITED STATES OF AMERICA

OPM   0 9 8 7 6 5 4 3 2 1

To Thomas John Pascal Wenk

Richard Griggs
Journal Entry for Mrs. Serson's Class

Hi, Mrs. Serson. When you gave us this journal assignment, I thought it was kind of stupid. Okay, *really* stupid. I'm still not all that into it. But here I go anyway.

The topic today is What's the Deal with Girls? A while ago I broke up with this girl, Liz. Things just didn't work out. No harm done, you know? But now when I see her in the halls, she gives me this look like I'm this huge jerk. I just don't get it. I mean, why can't she just get over it?

I know a lot of girls like me. And that's cool because I like a lot of girls too. But why do they have to be so nuts?

I hope that's journaly enough for you.

Larissa
Journal Entry for Mrs. Serson's Class

Sometimes I feel really smart. Like when my mom's doing the *TV Guide* crossword puzzle and she asks me a question like, "What's a Jim Carrey movie, seven letters?" And I just blurt out, *"The Mask,"* without even having to count the letters.

Other times I feel really stupid. Like when I'm sitting in math class. Or science class. Or French, or social studies . . . or pretty much any class besides gym and lunch. And lunch isn't really a class when you think about it.

Blue
Journal Entry for Mrs. Serson's Class

We hide, each in our own sweet darkness.
Does the other see?
Unable and unwilling to break free.

(Feeling kind of bummed out and poetic today. That's cool, right?)

Damon
Journal Entry for Mrs. Serson's Class

Late at night they rerun this TV show. It's called *CHiPS*, and it's actually kind of cool—in a cheesy kind of way. These two guys are cops, and they ride these big, old-fashioned motorcycles all over the place, and they always get the bad guy in some stupid, predictable way. I watch it every night. It's really good to fall asleep to.

Last night one of the cops, Ponch, got mad at his partner for stealing a girl he had his eye on, and he didn't talk to his partner for the whole episode until the partner saved his life at the end. It was pretty good.

Damon

"Damon? Would you please see me after class?"

The second I heard those words, my heart dropped. Mrs. Serson was asking me to stay after class? Me. Damon Ross. I always got good grades in English. The only person I'd ever seen Mrs. Serson keep behind was Rick Pierce, and that was because he'd spent the entire period carving four-letter words into the top of his desk. I must have done something really wrong. But what?

I tried to ignore the stares and giggles of the people around me as they headed for the hall and I approached my doom. I pulled my eyes from the floor for two seconds and risked a glance at Mrs. Serson. She was smiling. That was a good sign, right? Unless she enjoyed dropping the ax.

"Uh . . . hi," I said when I got to her desk. I stuffed my free, sweaty hand in the pocket of my jeans and found myself staring at her shoes.

Black shoes with little straps. Cool shoes for a teacher. Mrs. Serson was pretty cool in general. Young. Blond. Glasses that weren't attached to her neck by a beaded strap like every other teacher I'd had in my life.

Yep. She was cool. Except when she was keeping you after class.

"I want to talk to you about your journal," Mrs. Serson said, pulling off her glasses and looking me directly in the eye. She was a little taller than me, but she didn't stoop or bend over like some teachers do.

"What's wrong with it?" I asked, eyeing the blue notebook in her hand with my name neatly written across the top.

"There's nothing wrong with it, exactly," she said, leaning back against her desk and folding the book to her chest like she was hugging a teddy bear. "It's just not very personal." I felt my face burn up when she said that. I've never been very good at being personal or talking about my feelings, so you can imagine that having it pointed out to me made me majorly uncomfortable.

She flipped through the book quickly, scanning the pages. "You're obviously a talented writer," she said with a small smile. "Funny . . . descriptive . . . but the point is for you to write openly about your thoughts and feelings. I want all of my students to feel free to find their writing voice."

My writing voice? I was having a pretty hard time with my *actual* voice just about then.

"Do you understand what I mean?" she asked, holding the journal out to me. I looked down at the page she had opened to in the spiral. It was a list of my favorite breakfast foods, starting off with Lucky Charms.

I shuffled my feet.

"No more TV plots?" I said, slowly taking the book.

She laughed, but in a nice way, as if I'd made a joke instead of an awkward fumble.

"No more entries that aren't about you," she said. "I want to hear about what scares you, what makes you laugh, what motivates you. Try to think about that for tomorrow, okay?"

"Okay."

I turned and walked out before she could say anything else. All I could think was, *Okay. Right. Maybe in an alternate universe.*

Jessica

"I am so glad it's Friday, I could kiss the floor," I said as my sister and I stopped in front of her locker. Elizabeth and I both looked down at the dirty, scuffed, gum-wrapper-covered linoleum, and her face squished up.

"Please don't," she said, popping open her locker.

"Whatever," I answered. I leaned back against the locker next to hers and pushed my hair behind my ears. "So, I'm thinking about inviting Damon over to watch a movie tomorrow night."

Elizabeth's eyebrows immediately shot up, which I totally expected them to. I even knew exactly what she was going to say next. That's what comes from being practically joined at the hip for thirteen years. People who don't know us that well say we share the same brain. *That* is definitely not true. I can always tell what Elizabeth is thinking, but we never think the same way, if you know what I mean.

"Do you really think Mom and Dad will let you have a guy over to sit alone in the den?" she asked, pulling some notebooks out of her perfectly organized locker. Yep. Totally predictable Elizabeth-speak.

"Maybe," I said with a sly smile. "If you tell them you're going to be there too and then conveniently sneak back to your room." She probably knew I was going to say that too.

"Jessica—"

"Forget it," I said before she could get all Mom-like. She just rolled her eyes at me and straightened her pink-and-white-checked shirt before pulling her backpack onto her shoulders.

"It's just—"

"I said forget it," I repeated lightly. I knew if I pleaded and made enough promises, my mom would cave and let Damon come over. The real question was . . . "Damon will want to come, right?" I said, glancing at my reflection in her locker mirror and trying to sound like I was just asking to ask. Like I wasn't really worried he'd reject me to my face for no apparent reason.

Elizabeth looked at me like I'd sprouted a third ear. "Of course Damon will come."

"Are you talking about Damon Ross?"

My heart flopped as if I'd been caught doing something wrong. But when I turned around, all I saw was Elizabeth's weird friend Blue from the volleyball team. I guess he's not *that* weird, but I'm pretty much over the whole surfer-boy type. I like more serious guys . . . like Damon.

"Yeah, why?" Elizabeth asked.

"Because if you're expecting him to go any-where now, it's not gonna happen," Blue said, adjusting the strap of his ratty, sandy bag on his shoulder.

"What do you mean?" I said. What did this guy know about Damon?

He leaned in like he was going to tell some huge secret and looked each of us in the eye. I could smell the suntan lotion on him, and I wondered if he went surfing before school. How anyone could get up that early was be-yond me.

"Well?" I prodded.

"Mrs. Serson kept the dude after class," Blue said, glancing over his shoulder toward the classroom in question. "Totally bogus. He looked pretty bummed, so I guess he's in trouble."

Suddenly I felt just a little nauseous. I looked at Elizabeth, and she was doing the whole concerned-wrinkled-brow thing she has down pat. I couldn't believe Damon was getting kept after class. As if he didn't have enough to worry about with his sisters and his mom working all the time and that new boyfriend of hers—Ben.

I looked down the hall toward his English class, but he still hadn't come out. Things did not look good.

Lacey

I was in the most heinous mood ever. I kept trying to tell myself that it was Friday and I should be happy, that I was done with this smelly, loud, suffocating place for a whole two days. But no matter how I tried, I could not make myself feel better. Even stalking down the hallway with a look on my face that made all the seventh-graders practically jump out of my way was doing nothing for my mood.

"What's your problem?" Bethel McCoy said, falling into step next to me.

That kind of comment was *not* going to help.

"Let's see," I said, rounding a corner. "Mr. Wilfred bawled me out in math class when I was one of about ten people who didn't do the homework, Anna Wang slammed her locker door on my *hair* in gym today and ripped out a chunk the size of a golf ball, and I just snagged my favorite sweater on the door of Mrs. Ryan's room."

I flung out my arm to show her and whacked

some kid on the back. He tripped over his own feet and hit the deck. It almost made me laugh. *Almost.*

"Sorry," Bethel told the kid as he practically crawled away. She turned and gave me a look of death. Why? Because I didn't apologize to some kid I didn't even know? It wasn't like I *meant* to do it. And I was a little distracted at the moment.

"You need a serious attitude adjustment," Bethel said, pushing her straight black bangs out of her face.

I rolled my eyes and started walking again. "What I *need* is a peaceful afternoon away from this stupid school," I said, taking another corner.

That was when the fourth monumentally sucky thing of the day happened to me. I slammed right into someone. I dropped flat on the floor on my butt, and all my books went flying. And when I looked up to see who the loser was who'd gotten in my way, I found myself staring into the smirking eyes of Richard Griggs—Sweet Valley Junior High's most conceited jerk.

"Great," I said, pounding the floor with my fist. Bethel already had half my books in her hands. "Don't you watch where you're going?" I growled, glaring up at him.

Richard ran a hand through his thick brown hair and shifted his weight from one foot to the other like he was in the middle of a Paris runway instead of a cramped hall in a dingy school in the middle of a no-name town.

"Maybe I was just blinded by your beauty," he said, giving me a totally obnoxious wink.

"I have to go," Bethel said, handing me my stuff and bailing before I could even blink. Couldn't blame her, though. Not many people could hold their lunch in the presence of that much cheese.

I decided I couldn't even waste time coming up with a response for a stupid line like the one Richard had just laid on me, so I brushed myself off and started to get up. Richard bent over and grabbed my wrist, hoisting me off the ground before I could resist. I flung him off the second I was fully standing.

"Lacey, relax. I . . ."

"What?" I spat. I'd barely ever even talked to the guy, and now he was getting cozy?

"Chill!" he said smoothly, raising his hands. Then he took a step toward me and lowered his chin. When he looked at me that way, I could *maybe* see why people thought he was cute. But I was so not interested. I already had Gel, and he was almost more than I could handle. "I'm sorry

I bumped into you," Richard said in this low voice. But he was still smiling, like he was amused or something.

I was about to tell him off again when I saw Elizabeth Wakefield come around the corner and freeze in her tracks. The wide-eyed thing she was doing reminded me that she'd briefly dated Richard, and I can never resist making a Wakefield squirm. I leaned toward Richard slightly and touched his arm. "Well, I guess everybody makes mistakes," I said, blinking up at him.

Richard's smile widened. Over his shoulder I could see Elizabeth scurrying past us, looking completely crushed. It was just too easy.

Richard crossed his arms over his chest. "So do you want to—"

"Save it," I said. There was no reason to stick around now that Elizabeth was gone. I took one moment to catch the surprised look on Richard's face before I spun around and left him in the dust. This day was already improving.

Elizabeth

"I got it!" I yelled for about the fiftieth time. And for about the fiftieth time I didn't, in fact, get it. The volleyball went whizzing by my face and missed my fisted hands by about four inches. I couldn't hit the ball to save my life, and I was irritated by my own clumsiness. But what was even more irritating was the reason I was totally clumsy.

Richard Aaron Griggs.

And Lacey Frells.

"What's your deal today?" Marlee Randall said, slamming the ball against the floor and then catching it with both hands. She gave me her all-attitude look along with a sharp jerk of her head that sent her curls bouncing in front of her face.

"Sorry," I said, glancing guiltily at the rest of my team. "I'm just a little out of it." A couple of people shrugged, but the only one who smiled was Blue Spiccoli. You can usually count on Blue to be laid-back and carefree. I wish I could be

16

more like him sometimes. Right now I was not even close. My neck was all tight, and I could feel my teeth clenching. The thing was, I was over Richard Griggs. He was a jerk. A moron. He was totally useless.

So why was I feeling so terrible?

Suddenly the whistle blew. I had barely even noticed we'd had another volley.

"That's all for today, kids!" Leaf said, clapping. He shot me a reassuring glance, and I knew he wasn't upset about my performance. Thank goodness. I was surprised he wasn't ready to drop-kick me out the door.

"Hey, Wakefield!" Blue called out as he jogged across the gym. I tightened my ponytail and tried to ignore Marlee whispering to her friend Diva about how bad I was.

"What's up?" I asked, feeling irritable. I do like Blue, but all I wanted to do right then was head home and take the longest shower ever.

He patted me on the back and quickly squeezed my shoulder. "A bunch of us are going to chill on the beach by my house. Wanna come with?"

I felt bad about turning him down, but at that moment the last thing I wanted to do was hang out with the people I'd just humiliated myself in front of. "I don't think so, Blue, but thanks."

Elizabeth

"C'mon," he said, his blue eyes looking right into mine. Blue has kind eyes. And he always really listens. Unlike Richard Griggs, who's always looking over your shoulder to see if there's someone cooler to talk to behind you. "Think about it. The sound of the waves crashing into the shore. Seriously soothing."

I felt a blush creep up my cheeks from just knowing that my emotions were so transparent. I grabbed my gym bag and water bottle. "I really have to go home," I said. "I'll see you tomorrow." Then I turned as quickly as I could and walked out, trying not to think about the disappointed look on Blue's face.

Damon

"Damon! Don't forget to jiggle the handle or the—"

"Water will run hot! I know!" I finished my mom's sentence for her as I rushed to the bathroom with my little sister Kaia's dress. She'd just dumped half a cup of fruit punch all over the skirt. It was one of the few hand-me-downs from my other sister, Sally, that hadn't been stained beyond belief when it had been *Sally's*. I had to save it.

I jiggled the handle and stuck the dress under the stream. As I scrubbed at the stain, Kaia toddled in wearing nothing but a diaper and a smile. I looked down at her and smiled back. She might be a klutz, but she was still cute. She grabbed the leg of my sweatpants, pointed up, and said, "Damon spill!"

"No, Kaia spilled," I said.

"No! Damon spill!"

That was when I felt the water hit my socked feet. It took a few seconds too long for me to realize the sink was overflowing. But at least I stopped myself from saying something I'd regret saying in front of my baby sister.

"Mom!" I said loudly, turning off the faucet. "The sink's clogged again!" I hung the little dress over the shower rod and grabbed a semidry towel to mop up the mess. By the time my mom got to the bathroom, I was already bailing out the still water into the shower with a plastic cup.

"Great," my mom said, bringing her hand to her forehead. I handed her the cup and pushed past her.

"I'll go get the toolbox," I called. We'd done this so many times, it was like we were reciting lines by heart.

"Don't worry about it, hon," my mom said. That line was not in the script.

"Huh?" I said.

She walked by me and grabbed the phone from the kitchen. She was never out of my sight because our family lives in a trailer and you can pretty much see every inch of it from every other inch of it.

"Ben's an expert at this type of thing, remember?" she said, dialing a few numbers. "Maybe he can fix it once and for all."

Ben is my mom's boyfriend, and I held my breath at the sound of his name. I felt like I did when I was little and someone took my favorite toy away—which really didn't make much sense. I mean, I'm all for having the sink fixed once and for all. But it was just that I always fix the sink when it breaks. Just like I always oil the hinges and patch the leaks in the roof. And now Ben was going to come over and take care of it.

It was like I was being . . . replaced.

Lacey

"We're gonna go play Road Rash," Gel told me, leading the way through a stream of kids.

"Oh, yeehaw," I muttered at his leather-covered back. If someone had asked me what I really wanted to do on Saturday night, I can tell you exactly what my answer wouldn't have been. It wouldn't have been, "I'd love to watch Gel and his idiot friend Rob scarf down greasy pizza at Guido's and then play motion-sickness-inducing games all night at the Astro Arcade while ten-year-olds play tag all around me."

That definitely wouldn't have been the answer. So why was I here? Why did I find myself following Gel and Rob over to a line of big-screen games with fake motorcycles you could actually sit on? Because I had nothing better to do, that's why. And I was sick and tired of having nothing better to do. I wanted some excitement. Something other than the grunt-and-shrug routine Gel had mastered about a month into our so-called relationship.

Gel was busy revving up his fake motor when I saw him. Richard Griggs—the answer to my boredom. He was over by the far wall, shooting hoops at one of those little basketball simulators while a couple of his friends watched. He was wearing this tight, gray, V-necked T-shirt, and his hair was flopping in his face. I had to admit he was looking good.

The guy was annoying. The guy was conceited. But hey, like I said, I was really bored.

"I'll be right back," I told Gel.

He grunted. And shrugged.

I rolled my eyes and made a beeline for the guy with the pulse.

"Nice form," I said, walking up behind Richard. He missed the next shot. I smirked.

"Thanks," he said, looking me up and down. I knew I looked *good* in my new blue dress. Good enough to make him miss the next few shots. But he didn't. He hit them perfectly. *Swish. Swish. Swish.* I felt a blush rise to my cheeks, which was too annoying.

"Yeah, you should really try out for the minibasketball team," I said, leaning against the game next to his, which had a ripped sign on it that read Out of Order. One of his friends let out a chuckle. Richard eyed me again, and I shot a look at Gel, hoping he was catching this.

23

Making him jealous would be an added bonus. Of course, he wasn't paying any attention. Fine. If I wasn't in the room to him, he wouldn't be in the room to me. I turned my back on Road Rash and focused my full attention on Richard.

"So," he said, picking up a stack of tokens. "Think you can beat me at Skee Ball?"

I grabbed a few of the tokens out of his hand. "I can beat you at anything," I said.

Then he smiled at me and laughed. And suddenly I had to get out of there. "Thanks for the tokens," I said, struggling to keep the sarcastic grin on my face as I spun around, twirling my skirt perfectly.

It took Richard a second to recover, but then he shouted after me, "My pleasure, Frells."

I didn't even look back.

Richard on Lacey

I've decided Lacey Frells is different than all the other girls at school. Some people may say she's bad different. Like she's obnoxious and mean. And I guess sometimes she *is* mean. But at least she's not nice to your face and mean to you behind your back, like a lot of other people. She's different in other ways too. She doesn't get all giggly when you look at her. And she talks back instead of just uming and uhing. She doesn't let anyone push her around. And you can tell that she's not going to agree to have pizza just because you want pizza. In fact, if she knew you wanted pizza and she *really* wanted pizza too, she'd probably say she *didn't* want pizza just to be a pain in the butt. Just to keep things interesting. Just to be herself.

That's kinda cool.

Jessica

"So, how was school yesterday?" I asked Damon as I plopped down next to him on the couch in my den. My parents had agreed to let him come over without so much as a warning to be good. I guess when I don't get in trouble for a few weeks, they forget how easily I usually get in trouble.

"School?" Damon asked, doing that little eyebrow-raise thing that is too adorable to describe. "Why would I want to talk about school on a Saturday night?"

"Good point," I said with a little fake giggle. I leaned my head on his shoulder and looked at the TV so that he wouldn't be able to see my face—which was confused and disappointed. We were supposed to be boyfriend and girlfriend, right? So why was he still keeping secrets from me? Why hadn't he told me that Mrs. Serson had kept him after class?

There had to be some way to get him to talk about it. Suddenly I had an idea.

"I got a C on an English test," I lied. We hadn't gotten anything back in English class, but maybe the mention of the word . . .

"Really?" Damon said, looking down at me. "On what?"

"A quiz," I said quickly, shifting so that my chin was now on his shoulder and I was looking into his puppy-dog eyes. "In *English*."

"Well, that's not too bad," he said, brushing my hair back from my face and sending a chill down my side. "Quizzes don't count for much."

"No. I guess not," I said, disappointed. He kissed my forehead. For a second it made me forget I was supposed to be grilling him for information. Damon just had that effect on me. I put my head back on his shoulder and decided to leave it alone. He obviously wasn't going to say anything. And the more I tried, the more annoyed I was going to get, and then I was going to have a bad night. I almost smiled. My logical train of thought had *Elizabeth Wakefield* written all over it. I guess I'd listened to her advice so many times, it had finally started to sink in.

"Hey, guys!"

Elizabeth picked that exact moment to come bouncing into the room with her two

27

little sidekicks, Anna Wang and Salvador del Valle.

"Ooh, are we interrupting something?" Salvador asked, waggling his eyebrows in that way that he thought was funny but was really just stupid.

"No," Damon and I both said at the same time. We quickly moved apart as if my parents had walked into the room. That's the effect the responsible twin sometimes has on you.

"What are you guys watching?" Anna asked, grabbing off the table the bowl of popcorn I'd popped myself.

"*She's All That*," Damon answered, moving closer to me again so that Salvador could sit down at the end of the couch. As Damon's shirt rubbed against my cheek, I realized it was the first time I'd ever wanted to thank Salvador for anything.

"Ugh! I hate this movie!" Anna groaned. She grabbed a handful of popcorn, held it in her hand in a ball, and then munched on it like it was an apple. Totally gross.

"Ick, Anna," I said.

"She can't eat finger food one by one," Elizabeth said, sitting on the big, comfy chair and crossing her legs in front of her. "She has this *thing* about it."

28

"Whatever," Anna said. "At least I'm not afraid of mustard." She dropped onto the floor and glanced over at Salvador with a smirk.

"You're afraid of mustard?" Damon asked, his head snapping away from mine so he could face Salvador.

"Petrified," Elizabeth answered for him gleefully.

"Long story," Salvador said, slamming his long legs down on top of the table. "But it's not as bad as the reason Anna hates this movie."

"Why?" I asked, my heart suddenly feeling heavy. I tried to ignore it, but I knew I wasn't going to be able to.

"Because she hates Freddie Prinze Junior's eyebrows!" Elizabeth and Salvador yelled at the same time.

Damon laughed and leaned back in his seat, and I forced a smile. But inside I had this sinking feeling. Anna, Elizabeth, and Salvador obviously knew so much about each other. Why wasn't it like that with Damon and me? He didn't even tell me about major life events like getting in trouble in English, but Elizabeth knew about Salvador's food phobias. They both knew about Anna's eyebrow hang-ups. And none of them were even *dating*. I looked up at Damon's profile and sighed.

Jessica

Didn't he care about me enough to let me in on his life?

Maybe things with Damon weren't as perfect as I'd thought.

Damon

"Where do you guys keep the salt?" Ben asked on Sunday night as he and my mom made dinner in the tiny little space we like to call the kitchen.

"Behind the sugar," Mom and I answered.

I didn't even look up from Sally's homework paper. I'd been helping Sally with her homework since she started school. That's what happens when your mom works crazy hours. Not that I minded. I kinda liked the way Sally looked up to me.

"Damon," my mom said in her I'm-about-to-get-on-your-case voice. I glanced over at her. She was sweating a little from working over the stove, and she had a piece of her brown hair stuck to her forehead. "Don't you have any of your own homework to do?" she asked.

"No," I said, shifting in my creaky metal chair. "I did it all already." I quickly ran through my schedule in my head. Science, check. History, check. Math, check. English . . . oh no.

"Ugh!" I groaned and lowered my head to the table.

"Ugh, what?" my mom asked, hovering above me.

"I forgot I have some . . . writing to do," I said, running my hands through my hair. I didn't want to tell my mom we had to keep a journal for English because she'd probably want to read it—you know, see into my head and all that. Of course, according to Mrs. Serson, I wasn't accomplishing that inner-voice thing, so I guess it wouldn't really matter.

Ben walked up next to my mom, wiping his hands with a dish towel. "So why don't you go do it?" he said. "I can help Sally with her homework while your mom finishes dinner."

"Yeah! Ben can help!" Sally said with her cute smile.

My insides immediately started to squirm, and I looked down at the page with all the nice, big numbers written out on it. *Chill out,* I told myself. *He's just trying to help.* Unfortunately, part of me really didn't want his help. Part of me wished he would just go away so Sally would need *me* to help her.

"That's okay," I said, stroking Sally's hair. "I can do my work after dinner."

"But if you do it *before* dinner, we can all play a game together *after* dinner," my mom said, stirring the spaghetti sauce on the stove.

"Yeah! Can we play Candy Land?" Sally exclaimed. She leaned hard against the table and blinked up at me. "Damon? Can I be yellow?"

I narrowed my eyes at my mom. I couldn't believe she'd played the board-game card. That was so unfair.

"Go on, Damon," Ben said, picking up a pencil. "I've got it covered."

My heart was pounding, but I couldn't think of a good excuse to stay there, so I made myself get up from the table. It was so weird—like I could hardly pull myself away. But when Ben took my seat, there was really no room for me anyway.

Larissa
Journal Entry for Mrs. Serson's Class

Last night I went to a movie with a few of my friends. We had the best time. We laughed and talked and threw popcorn at each other and one of the ushers had to shush us about three times. It was so great. I wish life could always be like that. I wish I could always hang out with my friends and do the things I want to do.

No offense, but why does school always have to get in the way?

Damon
Journal Entry for Mrs. Serson's Class

On Friday our sink broke—again. Normally this wouldn't be a topic worth writing about. Normally I'd just fix it and clean it out, and everything would be fine. But this time I didn't have to fix it because Ben did. Ben is really good at fixing things. *He's* good at a lot of stuff.

Ben, in case you're wondering, is the guy my mom's dating. And I don't know why, but the fact that he's so good at everything makes me mad. I mean, I should be happy that he's such a great guy. And I *am* happy. I'm happy my sisters have a father figure now because I'm sure I was really bad at that. And I'm happy that my mom seems happy. So it's good that Ben's around.

Really good.

Elizabeth

I'd just found a totally comprehensive list of Earth Day events that I needed for my science project after hours of surfing the Web when Jessica came trudging into my room. I was thankful for the interruption—I hadn't been feeling all that into what I was doing anyway. I reached for the mouse and book-marked the page just in case. There was no telling what could happen when Jessica was around. The girl could lean over the keyboard and click onto a makeup Web site in about two-point-five seconds.

I swiveled in my chair, took one look at Jessica, and realized liquid eyeliner wasn't the first thing on her mind. "What's up?" I asked, forgetting about the computer the second I saw the little lines etched on her forehead.

"Nothing." She sighed dramatically, flopping onto my bed. She flung her arms out to her sides and stared up at the ceiling, her eyes all droopy.

"Jess, come on. Just spill," I said. She sighed again.

"Damon doesn't tell me anything," she blurted out, keeping her eyes on the ceiling.

"Is this about the English-class thing?" I asked. I pushed my chair over the thick carpeting and propped my feet up on my bed.

"Yes!" she said as if I'd asked the most obvious question ever. "Well, kind of. It's just that he doesn't tell me anything. You and your friends know everything about each other, and I don't even know, like, Damon's favorite color."

I took a deep breath and leaned back in my chair. "Jess, Damon's different than Salvador and Anna," I said, picking at a little string on the hem of my shirt. "He's not as open. He doesn't . . . *share* as much."

"Great," Jessica said, throwing up her hands and letting them slap back onto my pink-and-white bedspread. "So you're saying I'm just gonna have to deal with Secretive Guy?"

"Not necessarily," I said. I tilted back my head so I was staring at the ceiling too. "Just give him some time. He really likes you. He'll come around."

Jessica was quiet for a few seconds. And that never happened. Especially when we were talking about her. I lowered my head, and a head rush grayed my vision for a moment, but when I could see again, she was giving me a confused look.

"What?" I asked.

"What's wrong with *you?*" she asked, scrunching up her face. "You're acting all . . . distracted."

I took another deep breath and let it out slowly. I hadn't even realized it, but she was right—I *was* distracted. "I saw Lacey flirting with Richard Griggs," I admitted.

Jessica sat up straight, her hair swinging over her shoulder and landing perfectly. Like it always did. Mine never did that, even though we have basically the same hair. "You're kidding. Lacey Frells and Richard Griggs?"

Why did hearing her say that make my heart squeeze? "Yeah, and for some reason, it really bothers me, even though I am *totally* over him," I said, standing up.

"Of course it bothers you," Jessica said. She pushed herself off the bed. "Lacey is the most annoying person on the planet." She crossed her arms over her chest. "I wouldn't worry about it, though. She's probably just using him like she did Damon."

"That's the thing. I don't care if Lacey likes Richard or not. I wouldn't care if she was *marrying* Richard," I said, covering my face with my hands. This feeling was so frustrating because I just didn't know what it meant. It was like a tightness in my chest every time I thought about the two of them, which felt like jealousy. But it couldn't be. "Why do I feel this way when I have absolutely no interest in either one of them?" I asked, not really expecting an answer.

"Maybe you're just jealous Richard found someone first," Jessica said matter-of-factly. "Maybe you wanted to find someone and rub his face in it before he could." She shrugged and looked at her nails. "It's perfectly natural."

I wanted to tell her she was insane. That that would be a totally immature response, and there was no way that was the reason I felt so lousy. Only when I thought about it, I realized with a sickening thud in my stomach that she could actually be right. And that was really unfair.

Lacey

So, the weekend had pretty much been a bust. Gel was his usual idiot self, my stepmonster had forgotten to pick up my Honey Nut Cheerios, so I had nothing to eat on Saturday morning, and it had been cloudy all day Sunday, so the tan was rapidly waning. But Monday was looking good, partly because *I* was looking good. I'd already caught at least three guys checking me out, and I was feeling really confident.

Then I made the mistake of opening my locker. And there, sitting on top of my normal jumble of notebooks, balled-up gym clothes, and CDs I'd long since forgotten about, was a folded-up note. One of those specially folded-up notes that's creased into a tight little square so it's hard to open. So it's top secret. Majorly cheesy.

I grabbed it and practically ripped it open. All I had to do was scan it and see the words *amazing, you, I, smile,* and the signature, *Richard,* and I was redder than a tomato. I slammed my locker and stalked toward the ninth-grade lockers. Richard was just standing there, chatting with a couple of friends, like he'd never written a thing. But I wasn't about to let him off the hook. He'd already ruined my perfect Monday with his stupid note.

"Do not write me love notes," I spat, flinging the paper at his chest. It hit him and plummeted to the floor. He and all his little friends looked at it for a second, and then they all cracked up laughing—everyone except Richard.

"All right, guys, ha ha," Richard told them, pulling me aside. "Move along." And they actually did. That's the kind of persuasive power Richard had. Well, not with me. He turned his smiling eyes on me. "Lacey—"

"No!" I said, raising my hand to stop him. "Who do you think I am, Elizabeth Gullible Wakefield?" He snapped back his head a little as if he couldn't believe I'd brought her up. "I'm not going to fall for your usual little act—"

"Lacey." His face was suddenly unbelievably close to mine. "There's nothing usual about this."

That was when I forgot what I'd been saying. I swear, when I looked into his eyes, I could actually almost believe he was being sincere. That he really liked me. And it's not like guys don't like me, because they do. But I knew guys like Richard. They went out with a million girls and told each one of them they were more special than the last. Well, I, for one, was not that naive. And Richard Griggs was not *all that*.

So why did I feel so out of breath?

I had to get out of there.

"Richard, get this straight. I am not interested in you. And I'm definitely not interested in your games. So just leave me alone, okay?" Then, with a final groan that definitely showed my total frustration and disgust, I turned and stormed away.

Richard's Note

Dear Lacey,

I just wanted you to know that I think you're amazing. Sounds stupid, right? *Amazing*. But it's the only word I could think of to describe you, and your attitude, and your smile. You don't use that smile nearly enough.

I wish you would.

Richard

Damon

Mrs. Serson excused the class and all the chairs around me scraped back. Books were slapped shut. Bags were thrown over shoulders. Sneakers started squeaking on the floor. But I didn't move. I just stared at the cover of my journal, trying to figure out if there was a way to get by Mrs. Serson without turning it in.

"Damon?" Mrs. Serson said.

Guess not.

I looked up, and the room was pretty much empty. There was no turning back now. I picked up my stuff and slowly approached the front of the room. Mrs. Serson gave me one of those reassuring smiles teachers are always giving. But *she* didn't make it seem like she was looking down at me. Like I was a kindergartner. She was good that way.

"Here you go," I said, holding out the journal.

"Thanks, Damon," she said. "I'm looking forward to reading it." And then she just took it and slipped it into her bag.

My knees almost gave out. I didn't really know if I wanted her to read what was in there, but what was I going to do—steal her bag? It looked like I was just going to have to live with the fact that someone was going to know all about my screwed-up life.

Jessica

"Anna and . . . Samantha . . . ," Mr. Taffe said, placing two little slips of paper aside on his desk. I hated this kind of thing—when teachers matched us up with project partners at random. Like we weren't capable of picking work partners ourselves. It was just insulting.

"Jessica and . . ."

My heart stopped. *Just don't let me get hooked up with a dork,* I thought.

"Chris Grassi," he said.

Chris Grassi? Hmmm. I glanced over my shoulder at my new partner, and he grinned at me. The boy had perfect teeth. In fact, he had perfect blue eyes, and perfect blond hair, and perfect taste in clothing too. He was one of the cutest guys at SVJH, and he hung out with all the jocks. He was also the highest scorer on the basketball team. He was the textbook definition of a total babe.

I smiled back and then turned around in my seat, but even though Mr. Taffe had started lecturing about chromosomes, I couldn't stop smiling.

"What's the dopey grin about?" Bethel whispered, leaning across the aisle. "Psyched to be hooked up with blondie over there?" She tilted her head toward the back of the room, where Chris sat.

"Nope," I said, folding my hands on the desk in front of me. "Not at all."

Bethel rolled her eyes and slumped back into her seat. "Sometimes I just don't get you."

I picked up my pen and drew a little heart in my notebook, not bothering to explain myself to her. She wouldn't get it anyway. I was smiling because I'd realized that being paired with Chris hadn't affected me at all. That even though things weren't perfect with Damon, I still had no interest in anyone else. And that meant only one thing.

I really, *really* liked Damon.

Elizabeth

"Hey, Liz."

My heart hit my stomach at the sound of that voice, but I swallowed hard and managed to compose myself before I turned around. I knew that even if it was just my insides freaking out, Richard would be able to read my feelings on my face.

"Hey," I said. I put on a completely blank expression—like the one Jessica gets when you start talking about current events.

"Listen, can I ask you kind of a bizarre question?" He gripped his bag's shoulder strap with one hand, shoved the other in the pocket of his jeans, and leaned against the wall. He was so good-looking, he could have been a tear-out page in *Fourteen* magazine. Too bad he was such a ridiculously evil creep.

"I guess," I said, crossing my arms over my chest. I looked over his shoulder at the crowds walking behind him, just to show him how it felt to be ignored. But he didn't seem to notice.

"How well do you know Lacey Frells?" he asked.

"What!" Now I couldn't hide my irritation. Why was he asking me that? Was he trying to rub my face in the fact that he'd moved on? Why did he think I cared?

He shrugged like we were just talking about the lunch menu or something and looked me in the eye. "Well, I've seen her around your sister, and I just thought—"

"My sister?" I said, scrunching up my forehead. "My sister hates Lacey." His eyes widened, and I almost slapped my hand over my mouth, but I didn't. It was out there, and I couldn't take it back. Plus it was taking all my effort not to tell him what Jessica had told me—that Lacey was just using him the way she'd used Damon. She was probably only hanging around Richard to make that stupid high-school boyfriend of hers jealous. Part of me wanted to spit it out just to see his face. I mean, didn't he know that asking me this was going to hurt my feelings? Irrationally, I wanted to hurt his just as much.

But I didn't. That's just the way I am.

"Sorry, I can't help you," I said, taking a deep breath.

"All right. Whatever," he said, shrugging again. He pushed himself away from the wall

49

and looked me up and down. I thought he was about to say something else, but then he shook his head slightly and looked at the floor. "Guess I'll see you around," he said finally.

I glared at his back as he disappeared into the crowd. And I suddenly realized I'd never actually hated anyone before—until now.

Elizabeth on Why Guys Don't Matter

Guys are clueless. They don't think about other people's feelings. They don't think before they speak, and most of the time it looks like they don't even think before they put on their clothes in the morning.

They smell, they make fart jokes, they can't remember people's birthdays, but they know exactly how many home runs any given baseball player had last season. They never read unless it's a comic or a sports magazine. They never listen unless you're talking about cars or (again) sports. And they never say they're sorry. For anything. Ever.

Boys are definitely not worth the effort.

(There are exceptions to every rule, and I have to say that my brother, Steven, is an exception because if I don't, he'll give me an atomic wedgie.)

Jessica

Damon and I walked out of the lunch aisle and turned toward the insanely noisy cafeteria. Sometimes walking through that room with a full tray in my hands is more nerve-racking than coming to school with a bad haircut. There are too many opportunities for humiliation—tripping, spilling, bumping into someone and causing *them* to trip and spill. I took a deep breath and turned toward the table we usually shared with our friends.

"Why don't we sit over by the window today?" Damon asked from behind. Suddenly I forgot about the pitfalls of the lunchroom. The tables over by the window were smaller than the others. They were the tables where couples always sat—or kids who had no one else to sit with. Damon wanted me alone. Maybe he was finally going to tell me why Mrs. Serson had kept him after English class.

"Okay," I said. And within seconds we were

sliding into orange plastic seats in our own private little nook.

"You have to try this," Damon said, his eyes shining as he opened his brown-paper bag he brought from home and pulled out a big, chocolate-chip cookie.

"Damon, you rebel," I joked, ripping open my little milk carton. "Dessert before lunch?"

Damon grinned his heart-stopping grin and held out the cookie to me. "This is worth it. Here, try it."

I plucked the cookie out of his hand and took a little bite so there would be plenty left for Damon, but as soon as I tasted it, I wanted to scarf the whole thing. "That's amazing!" I said. "Did your mom make that?"

"No," Damon said, taking it back and biting a little off the other side. "But it's from her diner. If you really like it that much, I'll bring you your own tomorrow."

"Promise?" I said.

"Promise," Damon repeated. He broke what was left of the cookie in two pieces and handed the larger half to me. "Right now we're just gonna have to share."

"Thanks," I said, placing the rest of the cookie near the edge of my tray. I was going to save it for after I was done eating my lunch. It would give me something to look forward to while I was munching on meatball surprise.

While we ate, Damon told me a story about how his little sister Kaia had decided to eat red crayons for dessert last night, and before I knew it, half the lunch period had passed me by. I loved when Damon talked about his sisters. It was like he just lit up and couldn't stop talking.

"That must have been fun to clean up," I said with a laugh after hearing all the gory details.

"*Fun* isn't exactly the word I would use," Damon said, leaning back in his chair. "It was more like—"

"Hey, Jessica!"

I looked up to find Chris Grassi hovering next to our table, notebook in hand. Damon glanced from Chris to me and back to Chris. I could tell by the confused look on his face that he was wondering what the connection was. It's not like I'd ever mentioned Chris before.

"Hey, man," Chris said to Damon, lifting his chin in that way guys do when they're greeting each other.

"Hey," Damon said casually.

"So, Jess," Chris said, tossing his bangs out of his face—a gesture some girls would swoon over. "I didn't get a chance to talk to you after class. Do you have a minute to talk about our project?"

"Now?" I said, looking at Damon out of the corner of my eye. I was suddenly tense. What if he got jealous? What if he was upset because I was going to be spending time with one of the hottest guys in school? "Um—"

"Go ahead," Damon said, taking a bite of his sandwich. "You guys go talk. I have to go over my math homework anyway." He reached into his backpack and pulled out a fraying green notebook.

Okay. So apparently he wasn't upset.

"Cool. We can sit over there," Chris said, gesturing over his shoulder.

"Yeah." I gathered up my stuff and stood. "I'll talk to you later, Damon."

"Definitely," Damon said with a smile. I grinned back and turned to follow Chris to an empty table where we could have some relative privacy to talk. I was so relieved that Damon wasn't jealous. What a cool boyfriend.

Elizabeth

I was staring at the selection of lunch foods, wondering what I'd done to deserve such torture, when my new friend Rob from the volleyball team came up next to me. He put his tray down on the counter and adjusted the straps on his backpack.

"Hey," he said, staring at the plates in front of him.

"Can you believe this?" I said, throwing my hand out to indicate the steaming trays of muck. "Meatball surprise and tuna surprise on the same day. Do they think we're indestructible?"

Rob laughed, but in that way you laugh when you're just being polite or when you have something big on your mind. "Can I ask you something?" he asked, hooking his thumbs into the pockets of his chinos. I noticed his face was as pink as the stripe on the collar of his blue polo shirt, so I guessed he *did* have something big on his mind.

"What's up?" I asked, going for a prepackaged salad.

"Well . . ." He took a deep breath, and I glanced at him, confused. He was starting to make me nervous. "I saw what happened between you and Richard before, and I just wanted to tell you that if you're still upset about that jerk, you shouldn't be because he's a jerk and he doesn't deserve someone like you."

Wow. Guess he needed that big breath to get it all out.

"What do you mean, 'someone like me'?" I asked, filling up a cup with soda. Honestly, he couldn't be talking about what I thought he was talking about. Rob and I didn't know each other that well. He couldn't *like* me, could he?

"Look," he said, clutching his tray. "Every guy I know, including me, thinks you're one of the coolest girls at this school," he blurted out. "I mean, you're funny, you're pretty, you're nice to *everybody* . . . and I just think you can do better than Richard Griggs. That guy wouldn't know a cool girl if she walked right up to him and kissed him."

My mouth dropped open, and for a second I couldn't move. No one had ever said anything like that to me before. As far as I knew, no one had ever said anything like that to anyone I knew before. Ever.

"Not that I'm suggesting you do that," Rob

added finally. He was so red, I thought he was going to explode. He laughed a nervous laugh this time.

"Wow," I said, feeling like a huge weight had been lifted off my shoulders. "Thanks, Rob."

"No problem," Rob said with a shrug. "You don't think I'm a freak now, do you?" he said, the psychedelic color draining from his face slightly.

"No," I said honestly. "I don't think you're a freak."

"Good," he said. Then he bolted from the lunch line. Fast.

I wished he hadn't disappeared so quickly. Because I would have told him I hadn't felt this good in days. Three days, to be exact.

Damon

I left lunch early for two reasons.
One, I didn't feel like sitting by myself anymore, pretending to go over math homework I'd already gone over at home, and two, I didn't feel like watching Jessica and Chris hanging out at the next table anymore. As I walked down the deserted hallway, I kept telling myself there was no reason to be jealous of Chris. He and Jessica were just doing a project together. But as long as I've known Chris, he's always gotten every girl he wanted. And he's never cared whether she had a boyfriend or not. He's always snagged her anyway. So it was hard not to get a little paranoid. Because really, who wouldn't want Jessica?

That's what I was thinking when Mrs. Serson walked out of the teachers' lounge and knocked me right out of my depressing train of thought.

"Damon!" she said, holding her leather briefcase with both hands in front of her. "I just finished reading your journal entry."

Great. Just what I needed right now. More to worry about.

"I'm very impressed," she said, her eyes all shining. "I knew you just needed to open up a little. Your talent is even more obvious now."

I was probably about the color of a fire hydrant. "Uh, thanks," I said. *Way to go Damon. Really intelligent.*

Suddenly her brow wrinkled, and she looked past me down the empty hall. "Shouldn't you be in class?" she asked.

"I have lunch," I said, taking a step back. I could actually get detention for ducking out early. "I forgot something in my locker, so I was just going to get it."

Mrs. Serson smiled in that nice way I was getting used to seeing. "Well, then I'll walk with you," she said.

"Okay." And then we were walking down the hall together like two friends instead of a student and teacher. She could have demanded a hall pass or slapped me with detention, but instead she walked along at my side. It was almost too weird. But it was also kinda cool. Mrs. Serson definitely wasn't your regular kind of teacher.

"So, why don't you write for the *Spectator*?" she asked, her heels clicking and echoing against the shiny floor.

"I actually used to be on the staff, but I had to quit because I had to baby-sit practically every day," I told her. The second I heard myself say it, I blushed again. There was no way that information could have come out of me that easily. I'd spent over a year covering up the real reason I wasn't involved in any clubs or sports anymore, and now I'd just spilled it like it was last night's Lakers score.

Why was Mrs. Serson suddenly so easy to talk to?

"Do you still baby-sit that much?" she asked me as we turned the corner into the hall where my locker is.

My stomach dropped when she asked the question. Not because of the question, but because of the answer. And the reason for the answer. Ben.

"No," I said finally, shrugging as if it was no big deal, even though my insides were all jumbled. "Ben's there a lot, so my sisters don't need me as much."

"That's great," she said as I stopped in front of my locker.

I looked at the floor, completely uncomfortable. "Yeah. I guess."

"No, I don't mean it's great that they don't need you." She tilted her head a little to make me look her in the eye. "Which I'm sure they do." She just stared at me, so I nodded. "I meant it's great that you have free time because I'd love your help with something."

Now I was confused. A teacher wanted *my* help? This was a first. "With what?" I asked, twirling my lock.

Mrs. Serson popped open her briefcase and pulled out a sheet of paper. "I'm starting up a literary magazine, and I need a panel of students to help me. And I need someone to help me figure out how to get other kids interested." She handed me the paper and grinned. It said *SVJH Literary Magazine* across the top. I was totally confused. My teacher had obviously gone nuts. I mean, I knew she liked my one journal entry, but a literary magazine? As in poetry and essays and short stories? Was she kidding?

"You don't want me," I said, staring at the page. "I mean, don't you want someone like Liz Wakefield or something?"

"Nope." She snapped her briefcase closed, pulled out a long strap, and slung it over her shoulder. "Anyone will be welcome to make submissions, of course. But for the actual staff, I need people who are talented but who aren't involved in a lot of activities already. I want people who can focus on this."

Well, if she wanted someone who was uninvolved, she'd definitely picked the right guy. And with Ben around, I'd be able to give Mrs. Serson a lot of my time and energy. Which I suddenly wanted to do more than anything. It had been a long time since anyone had been so interested in anything I had to say. Except for Jessica, of course.

"Okay," I said, opening my locker and pulling out a notebook. I folded the paper and put it inside the notebook pocket.

Her whole face lit up like she had just won the lottery or something. "Great!" she said. "Our first meeting is today after school in my classroom." I checked my mental calendar and remembered that Ben was taking the girls to the mall that afternoon.

"Cool," I said, swallowing my jealousy at the thought of Ben buying Sally and Kaia their favorite ice cream at Casey's. "I'm in."

Jessica

I'd decided when I got up that I was going to skip track practice. Over the weekend I'd been doing yard work with my dad (can you say "yuck"?), and I'd stepped in a hole and twisted my ankle a little. (Can you say "child abuse"?) So I figured I had to let my ankle rest before running on it again. Now I just had to figure out what I was going to do with all that free time. I already had a good idea of who I wanted to spend it with.

After math class I caught up with Damon in the hall by his locker. I saw him before he saw me, and I took a second to just look at him. He was so nice to look at, after all. And he was mine. If I could only get him to open up, things would be perfect.

Anyway, I walked up to Damon and leaned against the locker next to his. "So," I said, flipping my hair over my shoulder. "What would you say if I told you I was going to buy you some serious pizza after school today?" I hugged my books to my chest.

"I'd say it sounds great, but I can't," Damon

answered, hardly even looking at me. Suddenly I was hugging my books harder and forcing myself to keep smiling.

"Oh," I said.

"Sorry, Jess," Damon said, pulling a few books out of the top part of his locker. He finally glanced my way, and I must have looked depressed even though I was trying so hard not to. "Really sorry," he said. "It's kind of a long story."

He slammed his locker and opened his mouth to talk. Maybe he was actually going to tell me the long story. Maybe he was going to *share*. And for a second I wasn't depressed anymore.

Then the bell rang.

Damon looked over his shoulder. "Ugh. I really have to go," he said. "I'll talk to you later." He kissed me quickly on the cheek and then basically sprinted away. So much for the long story. Or even the short version, for that matter.

I turned around slowly, staring at my shoelaces. I knew I probably looked about three years old, walking along with my head down, but I couldn't help it. I felt so dissed, and I didn't want anyone to read it on my face.

He probably has to watch his sisters or something, a little voice in my head reminded me. *You have to be understanding about that.* Which I was. All the time. But why would watching his sisters be a long story? What was going on? I knew the wondering was going to kill me.

"Jessica! Wait up!"

I turned around to find Chris Grassi jogging down the hall toward me. A couple of girls who were huddled nearby turned to stare at me when they heard him call my name. I lifted my chin a little. It was kind of cool that they were jealous. Even if there was no reason for it whatsoever. Chris and I weren't together, and we never would be, but it was still a much needed ego boost.

"What's up?" I said as Chris slid to a stop in front of me.

"Do you want to get together after school today to work on our project?" he asked.

Normally I put off work for as long as humanly possible. It's just the Jessica approach to learning. But it wasn't like I had anything *else* to do this afternoon.

"Sure," I said as he opened the door to our next class for me. "I'll meet you in the library."

"Cool," Chris said, grinning down at me as I walked past him into the room. "This is going to be fun."

Right, I thought, letting my hopes for an afternoon with Damon at a cozy little booth at Vito's erase themselves from my mind. *Science project with a total stranger. Fun.*

Lacey

"Lacey, how many times are you going to look at your watch?" my best friend, Kristin Seltzer, asked me as we stood outside by the parking lot on Monday afternoon. I'd glanced at my wrist about a hundred times already because Gel was supposed to pick me up right after school to take me home, and he was already ten minutes late. I kept noticing my leg bouncing in irritation, and I kept trying to stop it, but then a minute later I would notice it going again. If I didn't get home by four today, I was going to be grounded, pure and simple.

"Sor-*ry*. Am I annoying you?" I snapped at Kristin. She just rolled her eyes and smiled. That's what's so great about Kristin. I can get away with pretty much anything, and she still hangs out with me. Too bad for Gel *I* wasn't that easygoing with *him*. Strangulation was sounding good right about now.

"There's my mom," Kristin said as a silver BMW pulled up to the curb. She picked up her messenger bag and flipped her blond hair over her shoulder. "Are you sure you don't want a ride?"

I considered it for a second, but I didn't want her to know that I'd already given up on Gel. I was allowed to know what a jerk he was, but I didn't want anyone else knowing he was such a jerk. Even though I guess Kristin probably already knew.

"Nah," I said, concentrating on keeping my leg still. "He'll be here any second."

"Okay," Kristin said. She jogged over to her mom's car and glanced back. "I'll call you tonight."

I managed a wave before her mother peeled out of the parking lot. Kristin has a mother who does that kind of thing. Anything at all to get noticed. She's pretty cool.

Students continued to trickle out of the school, heading for buses and cars and bikes and the sidewalk, and there I was, standing alone like a . . . *loner*. I tried to look busy. I pulled out a notebook and looked engrossed. That lasted about five seconds. I filed my bright pink nails. I counted the cars in the parking lot. With each new, stupid time waster I felt my face growing hotter and hotter. I was starting to sweat, and my back was aching from standing up straight and looking nonchalant.

I found myself staring at the entrance to the parking lot. Glaring, actually. I got angrier with every car that came in that wasn't Gel's crappy Trans Am. It got to the point where I felt like I was just going to explode all over the gritty asphalt.

That was when I saw Richard Griggs. I let the breath I was holding puff out and quickly looked away. I felt the color drain from my face. The last thing I needed was to have Richard come over and start asking questions. And I knew he would. He'd been so *irritating* lately, and he didn't seem to take no for an answer. If he came over and asked me who I was waiting for and got that ridiculous smirk on his face like he knew what I was thinking, I was going to have a breakdown.

And I'm too young and cute for a breakdown.

I could feel him walking up behind me, but it was okay now because I'd finally gotten myself under control. I plastered a carefree look on my face and turned around, ready for whatever he had to say.

But when I whirled around, he wasn't there. He was yards off, walking away from the school with one of his friends.

Huh. He hadn't even seen me.

Damon

It felt really weird not to be running out of school when the bell rang. It had been a long time since I'd stayed after for any reason, and I'd forgotten how quickly the place empties out and how quiet it gets when there's just a club or a team here and there. I was grinning as I grabbed my backpack and jogged through the front hall toward Mrs. Serson's classroom. Being singled out for something like this still felt really good. I almost forgot about the fact that my sisters were going to spend the afternoon hanging out with Ben. Almost.

When I got to her room, Mrs. Serson had moved four desks into a kind of open square, and she was sitting at one of them. Jennifer Reed, a girl from my English class who answered pretty much every question ever asked, and Chelsea Sable, an eighth-grader I went to camp with when I was little, were seated at two of the other desks. Everyone looked up and smiled when I walked into the room.

"Hey," I said, catching my breath.

"Hello, Damon," Mrs. Serson said, gesturing at the empty desk. "Have a seat. Hope you don't mind hanging out with a bunch of girls."

My face reddened a little, but I played it off. "I can handle it," I said. Chelsea giggled. I didn't know her that well, but I knew she was a chronic giggler. And Jennifer was supposedly a brain.

"Okay," Mrs. Serson said as I settled into my chair. "Now that we're all here, let's get started. I want this literary magazine to be run by the students, *for* the students. That means we'll have an editorial board made up of seventh-, eighth-, and ninth-graders, and that board will exclusively select what does and doesn't make it into the publication. Now . . ."

As Mrs. Serson continued to talk about content, I pulled a notebook and pen out of my backpack. There was no way I was going to remember all of this if I didn't write it down.

"So what do you guys think?" Mrs. Serson said, looking around at each of us. "Should we have fiction, poetry, drama, photos? Maybe we should just ask for poetry in the beginning."

I raised my hand before I even realized what I was doing. Mrs. Serson's face lit up. "Yes, Damon?"

For a second I lost my voice and couldn't remember what I wanted to say. Why would any of these people want to hear my opinion about something like this?

"Feel free to speak your mind," Mrs. Serson prompted me. "It's what we're here for." I looked at Jennifer and Chelsea, and they were both watching me. They looked interested, so I cleared my throat and jumped in.

"Well, if you really want this to be for students, by students, why not let anybody submit anything they want?" I said, squirming slightly in my seat. "I mean, once we see what we get, we'll be able to tell what all the students are interested in writing, and that should tell us what they're interested in reading . . . you know?"

"Yeah!" Chelsea said, sitting up straight in her chair. She pushed her long, black hair behind her ears and blushed a little but kept talking. "And that way no one will feel left out just because they can't write poetry or something."

"Right," Jennifer added firmly. She made a little note on the pad in front of her, reminding me of a lawyer on one of those law shows I'm not supposed to stay up to watch. "I mean, just the word *literary* can be kind of intimidating, so limiting it to just poetry or just fiction would be even *more* intimidating."

"Good point," Mrs. Serson said, flipping through a bunch of loose papers in front of her and pulling out one that was already covered with chicken-scratch notes. She added something to the mess and looked around at us. "In fact, good points, all of you. I knew there was a reason I picked you guys to help me."

She smiled over at me, and I sort of swelled with pride. It's dorky, I know, but I couldn't believe where I was and what I was doing. I couldn't believe someone was listening to me. It felt great. Suddenly I had another idea.

"Maybe we shouldn't even call it a literary magazine," I said, glancing at Jennifer. "You know, because of the intimidating thing. *Sweet Valley Junior High Literary Magazine* sounds . . . snotty."

"Interesting," Mrs. Serson said, shifting slightly. I suddenly wished I hadn't opened my big mouth. What if I had offended her by calling her title snotty?

She narrowed her eyes a little as she looked at me, her pen held over her paper, ready to write. Then she smiled. Phew. "What would you call it instead?"

Now I was on the spot. My teacher was ready to write down whatever I said, and I'd spoken up before I'd thought it through. I had no idea what I'd call it. And I didn't want to suggest some dumb title that everyone would think was stupid.

"I don't know," I said, tapping my pen against the top of the desk so loudly, it seemed like the sound was bouncing around the room. Then it hit me. "How about *Our Voices*?"

"Yeah!" Chelsea said loudly.

"Definitely," Jennifer added, smiling.

Mrs. Serson was practically beaming. "All right, then," she said. "*Our Voices*, it is."

Lacey

When Gel's Trans Am finally pulled into the parking lot, I didn't move an inch. I just watched the car. Watched it pull through the first row of cars, go around an island, and screech to a rumbling stop in front of me. I didn't even flinch when the exhaust hit my face. Didn't cough.

Funny, I'd never been so angry I couldn't function before. Sure, this wasn't the first time Gel had flaked on me, but this was just too much. I couldn't take it anymore.

"Are you gonna get in or what?" Gel said, leaning across the passenger seat and shouting out the window. "I ain't gettin' any younger." That was when I snapped.

"You . . . you . . ."

"Me . . . me . . :," he mimicked.

My eyes blurred in front of me, but I was not going to cry. Not because of Gel. Not because I felt humiliated. Letting him see me cry would only make that humiliation worse.

Instead I forced a smirk onto my face and sauntered over to the open passenger-side window. I took a deep breath and leaned on the window frame. "Gel," I said, inhaling a little bit of the cigarette smoke that followed him around like Pigpen's dirt cloud. "You are so out of my life."

"What?" he spat, his face scrunching up in a horrible scowl. God, he wasn't even good-looking. He wasn't funny. He wasn't smart. He wasn't even *nice* to me.

"Where do you get off?" he shouted. As if he wasn't the one that was wrong. As if I wasn't the one who'd been standing here like an idiot for half an hour, thinking about what kind of punishment I was going to be slapped with when I got home. *If* I ever got home.

"I get off here," I shouted back. I mean, I couldn't let him get away with treating me this way. "God, Gel, you are such a loser!"

"Fine," he shouted. "Walk home!"

"I will!" I yelled back. "I'd rather walk to China than spend one more second in your presence."

"Whatever," he said, looking straight out through the windshield. "We're over—you clear?"

"Clear," I snapped.

He didn't even give me time to step back from the curb before he roared out of there.

"Ugh!" I groaned, squeezing my hands into fists. I couldn't believe what an idiot he was. I turned around to storm away, and then I realized people were staring at me. And I had no ride.

And Richard was back. I don't know why, but he was.

"I knew you wanted me," he said, hands in pockets, grin on face, hair flopped over forehead.

"*What?*" I snapped. Was this some kind of nightmare?

"You just broke up with your boyfriend," Richard said, gesturing in the direction Gel had raced off in. "Don't tell me that wasn't about me."

"Could you possibly be any more egotistical?" I said, crossing my arms in front of me. That was a little better.

"I could try," Richard said with a shrug. Still grinning. So irritating. A little breeze blew back his hair—perfectly timed, like he was in the middle of a photo shoot. It was like even nature loved him.

"Look," I said, shifting from foot to foot. "*That* was about the fact that Gel was supposed to be here half an hour ago to drive me home. And if I don't get there, like, pronto, I'm grounded. So unless you have a license and a pretty fast car, I suggest you leave me alone."

I grabbed my backpack from the ground where I'd left it, stalked over to the steps, and plopped down. Between fuming by myself, shouting at Gel, and screaming at Richard, I think I'd worn myself out. I just wanted to be alone to sulk and think, but Richard apparently wasn't done yet. He sat down next to me and propped his arms up on his knees. I opened my mouth to tell him off before he could say something more obnoxious than he already had, but when I glanced at his face, I stopped cold. He actually looked . . . concerned.

"I know you're pretty upset," he said, lacing his fingers together, "but I think I can help."

"Are you kidding?" I shot back. My heart was pounding, and I wasn't sure if it was because of him or because of all the drama. I was hoping it wasn't because of him.

"Well, you are acting like a huge jerk. But I'll help you anyway," he said, leaning his chin on the back of his hand.

Who did he think he was? I grabbed my backpack and jumped to my feet. But I hadn't gone three steps before I remembered I had nowhere to go. Reluctantly I turned, looked back at Richard, and took a deep breath.

"Yeah?" I mumbled. It took all my effort to get it out. "How?"

Richard looked out at the parking lot, breaking eye contact with me. "See that red station wagon right there?" he said. I looked over and saw the car in question. "That's my mom," Richard said. "And she just *loves* to drive pathetic waifs home."

I didn't know what to say. I couldn't even respond to the pathetic-waif comment. The red wagon that was now in front of us looked like a white chariot.

"Hey, Mom! Can you drive Lacey home?" Richard asked, standing.

Richard's mother looked me over as I stood, and she smiled. "Sure," she said. "If she's got cab fare and gas money."

Richard laughed and opened the back car door for me. Let me say that again. He *opened the back car door for me*. Unbelievable. Before I knew it, I was settled into a plush seat, listening to some oldies station, and on my way home.

All thanks to Richard Griggs.

Damon

When our meeting was over, Jennifer and Chelsea headed for the late bus, but I hung back to talk to Mrs. Serson. She packed up her stuff pretty quickly, and we walked out together, shutting the lights off behind us.

"So what's up, Damon?" she asked me. "Something on your mind?"

I shrugged and watched my battered sneakers as I walked. "I just wanted to say thanks for asking me to come," I said. "It was cool."

"You're welcome," she said, pushing through the double doors that led outside. "Thank you for coming. You had some great ideas."

As we strolled past the late bus, the doors slid shut and the engine rumbled to life. Mrs. Serson glanced at me, her brow knitted. "How are you getting home?"

"I usually walk," I said, looking out across the parking lot. It was a sunny, not too warm day, and it would be perfect for a long, slow walk home. Sometimes I get sick of having to walk home every day, but this day was different. This day nothing could possibly get to me.

Mrs. Serson stopped in front of a blue Ford and took out her keys. It was exactly the kind of car I would have expected her to have. Cute and conservative. Like her. I mean, she's not cute like Jessica's cute—she's cute like a mom's cute.

She leaned back against the car door, crossing her arms over her suitlike leather jacket. "I'm really glad you decided to get involved in this project, Damon. You're a really smart kid, and you have a lot to offer. You know that, right?"

"Yeah," I said shrugging. And at that moment I actually believed her. The more I hung out with Mrs. Serson, the more I wanted to hang out with her. Not only did she *listen* to me, but she also made me feel good. Like I was useful and . . . smart.

"So I'll see you tomorrow, then," Mrs. Serson said, opening the driver's-side door.

"I think I'm gonna call some of my friends that work on *Zone* and see if they want to contribute to *Our Voices*," I said out of nowhere. I think I just wanted to do more to keep the sort of high feeling I had going.

"That sounds great," Mrs. Serson said.

Damon

"See you tomorrow." I turned around and headed for the sidewalk. I couldn't wait to get home and get to work.

That was something I could honestly say I hadn't felt in a long time.

Jessica

"I think mold is the single greatest science project ever conceived of by man, woman, or child," Chris said, leaning back in the creaky library chair he hadn't sat still in all afternoon. He popped the end of his pen into his mouth and rolled it around, watching me and clearly waiting for me to ask why. I was ready and willing to ask. Chris had been cracking me up all afternoon.

"Why?" I said, doodling along the top margin of my notebook. "All you have to do is leave food out and let it get gross."

"You just answered your own question!" he said a little loudly for the library as he threw up his hands. He pulled the pen out of his mouth. "Minimal effort, maximum gross-out potential." I giggled, and he leaned forward in his seat. "I did it in eighth grade and actually made Lacey Frells barf."

"Really?" I squealed. Of course, I got a *shhh* from the librarian. I swear, Chris could probably run through the library naked and not get in trouble. That's how much of a golden child he is.

"Not a big Lacey fan?" he asked, raising his eyebrows.

"That's the understatement of the millennium," I said, leaning forward.

Chris looked me in the eye and crossed his arms on the table. "What else don't you like?" he asked in a serious whisper.

I just blinked. There it was again. That get-to-know-me tone. Aside from making me laugh, Chris had also spent the afternoon making me feel just a tiny bit uncomfortable. Like he was flirting or something. Didn't he know I was with Damon?

"I don't like science," I said, pulling my textbook toward me. "But that doesn't change the fact that we have to do this project." Nice, smooth change of subject, I thought. Apparently it didn't catch on with Chris.

"Forget the project. The project's boring," Chris said, slamming his book closed. "You're much more interesting."

I blushed big time. My hands were starting to sweat, and I was gripping the old, scratched cover of my book. "You know what? I have to make a phone call," I said, dropping the sweat-stained book and grabbing my purse.

"All right," he said, flipping open his notebook. "I'll just sit here being bored."

I took a deep breath and headed for the pay phone in the hallway. There was no way Chris Grassi was actually flirting with me. He could have any girl in school. Why would he waste time with someone who was already taken? I was obviously just on an ego trip, thinking he liked me. Which was making me feel guilty.

I dropped some change in the phone and dialed Damon's number, hoping Kaia wouldn't answer. The last time I got her, she talked about Barney for ten minutes before toddling off to find Damon. I mean, the kid's cute, but a person can take only so much fake-dinosaur-speak.

The phone rang twice and picked up.

"Hello?"

My brow knitted up. It was a guy's voice, but not Damon's.

"Hi . . . uh . . . Ben?" I said, hoping I was right.

"Yes?"

"This is Jessica Wakefield," I said. "Is Damon home?" I was already wondering why Damon had told me he couldn't hang out if he wasn't watching his sisters. Because if Ben was around, then Damon probably wouldn't have to be. It's amazing how fast my brain can work when I'm suspicious.

"No, he's not here right now, Jessica," Ben said. "Can I take a message?"

I found myself staring at all the phone numbers etched into the fake wooden box around the phone. If Damon wasn't home, where was he? What had he ditched me for?

"Yeah, can you just tell him I called?" I asked.

"Will do," Ben said.

I hung up the phone, feeling very, very awful.

Lacey

I was in the middle of a serious dilemma. I was sitting on the white couch in my white living room, and my little sister, Penelope, was asleep with her head in my lap (wearing, of course, a white dress). Our whole house is decorated in black and white because my stepmother is basically insane, but we won't get into that. Back to my current problem. Penelope was asleep, and the remote control was way out of my reach on the white-and-black coffee table, and *Saved by the Bell* had just come on the TV.

The question was, did I move and grab the remote, thereby waking up Penelope and forcing myself to listen to her whine for the rest of the night, or did I watch the single most annoying show ever to hit the airwaves?

The theme song was just coming to an end and I was about to rip out my eyelashes when the phone rang, and Penelope stirred. I dove for the remote, hit the 2 and the 4 for MTV, and grabbed the phone. The whining had already started before I could hit the talk button, but at least Screech hadn't gotten a chance to talk.

"Where's Mommy?" Penelope whined, her eyes barely opened.

I ignored her. "Hello?" I half whispered into the phone, hoping maybe there was a God and he would put Penelope back to sleep if I was quiet enough.

"Hey, is Lacey there?"

My heart skipped a beat in surprise. It was Richard. I could tell his smooth voice anywhere. How had he gotten my number?

"Why are you calling me?" I said.

He laughed. "I can tell by the obnoxious tone that I already have Lacey."

"Good call, brainiac," I said. "Are you going to answer my question?" What did he think, that just because his mother had dropped me off, he now had the right to call me whenever he felt like it? Did he think he was *in* with me now?

"I was just calling to say hey, you know," he said. I could practically see him shrugging on the other side of town. "Make sure you didn't get grounded."

There it was. The subtle reminder that he'd played the hero that afternoon. "Yeah, well, you've got *perfect* timing. My little sister *just* fell asleep, and now she's up again." It was a lie.

Penelope had fallen asleep a long time ago—long enough to put my leg to sleep by leaning on it—but he didn't have to know that.

"My timing was pretty perfect this afternoon," Richard said smugly. There was the *not* so subtle reminder of his heroism.

My face turned bright red as I remembered how he'd witnessed my little meltdown. It was so annoying how one day someone was barely even a blip on your radar screen, and the next day they were in your face every five seconds.

"I have to go," I said, knowing my voice sounded shaky, which was even more annoying.

"Wait. Lacey—"

The smoothness was gone, but I didn't care. I hung up before I could make a bigger idiot out of myself.

Lacey Frells's Ten Reasons
Why I Can't Like Richard Griggs

10. He's a player
 9. He dated a Wakefield
 8. He thinks he's too cool
 7. He wears argyle socks
 6. He . . . chews cinnamon gum . . . I think
 5. He . . .
 4. He . . .
 3. He . . .
 2. He . . .
 1. Fine, forget it. I just can't.

Damon

I was practically jogging by the time I reached the little walkway in front of my family's trailer. I'd spent the entire walk thinking about the magazine and how I was going to get people to participate. Elizabeth Wakefield was my best bet. If I could get her to submit some stuff, then all those people who wrote for *Zone* or wanted to write for *Zone* but hadn't would definitely send stuff in. It seemed like kids really looked up to Elizabeth and Anna and Salvador, and those kids would think *Our Voices* was cool if Elizabeth and her friends participated. Maybe *Our Voices* and *Zone* could even collaborate on stuff. *Our Voices* would focus on poetry and stories and stuff like that, and *Zone* would focus on news and current events.

This was going to be great. And Mrs. Serson was going to be so psyched when I told her I had a bunch of recruits.

I swung open our semiflimsy front door, all pumped up, and the smile dropped from my face the second I looked inside. I had actually forgotten about Ben. For a little while anyway.

"Hey, Damon!" Ben said as I walked into the room. My sisters didn't say anything. They didn't even look up. I guess they were too absorbed with what they were doing—which was spreading peanut butter on a stack of saltine crackers.

"Hey," I said, standing awkwardly by the door. All of a sudden I felt out of place in my own house. "What are you guys doing?" I asked, placing my backpack on the floor next to me.

"We're making Mommy a snack for when she comes home from work," Sally said, holding up a cracker glopped with peanut butter.

Great, I thought. *One more thing I used to do for my mom that Ben suddenly decided was his responsibility.*

"Wanna help?" Kaia added, licking her fingers. She seemed to have gotten more peanut butter on her face, hands, and arms than she had on the crackers. I felt my lips start to lift at the corners. You could always count on Kaia to make a mess. And to eat everything in sight.

I looked over the cozy little threesome. There didn't seem to be a single inch of room in which to squeeze myself. "That's okay," I told Kaia. "It looks like you've got it covered."

Ben glanced at me and held my gaze for a moment. I could tell he'd heard something in my voice. Even though I hadn't planned on sounding bitter, it had come out that way. And now it was just sort of hanging in the air as we looked at each other and the girls kept working, oblivious. It felt like we were having a kind of staring contest like a couple of second-graders. Good to know my mom's boyfriend was so mature.

Of course there was no way *I* was going to look away first.

"I should probably get going," Ben said finally, rubbing a hand over his stubbly chin. He glanced down at Sally, and I couldn't help smiling in triumph. I wiped my hand over my mouth and got rid of the little smirk before he looked up again. I knew I was acting like a bratty kid, and I wasn't proud of it, but around Ben, I sometimes couldn't help it. He was just so . . . in my face all the time.

After saying good-bye to the girls, Ben grabbed his jacket off the arm of the couch and walked toward the door. I stepped out of his way so he could leave, but he paused when he was next to me.

Just go, I thought.

"You going to be okay getting them cleaned

up and tucked in?" he asked, slipping his arms into his denim jacket.

My hands clenched. I couldn't believe he had asked me that. As if I hadn't done it a million times before. Of course it would be a lot easier if he hadn't let them roll around in peanut butter, but it wasn't like I was going to say *that*.

"I'll be fine," I told him, stuffing my hands under my arms so he wouldn't see the fists. There was that sarcastic tone again. Two months ago I wouldn't have even known how to sound sarcastic. I guess Ben brought out the worst in me.

He narrowed his eyes and opened his mouth to say something, and I was immediately filled with dread. The last thing I wanted was to get into a discussion with him right now. But Kaia suddenly flew across the room and flung her arms around Ben's leg.

He laughed and tousled her hair. "What's up, Kaia?" Ben asked. I could almost kiss her for distracting him at that crucial moment.

"I want *Ben* to tuck us in!" Kaia shouted.

At that moment my heart pretty much stopped beating. My sister was actually choosing Ben over me. To my face.

She's only two years old, I reminded myself. *She doesn't know any better.* But that thought didn't make it hurt any less.

"Yeah, Ben, stay," Sally added, twisting the knife a little deeper. What was this, a mutiny?

Ben glanced at me quickly and then removed Kaia from his leg. "I have to go, you guys," he said, reaching for the doorknob. "But I'll see you tomorrow."

Kaia stomped back to the couch, peanut-buttery arms crossed over her chest, and flopped down to sulk. At least she wasn't throwing a full-out temper tantrum. Sulking was a lot easier to deal with.

Ben took a deep breath and let it out slowly, staring at the floor with his hand on the door. All I could do was hope he wasn't going to say what he'd been trying to say a minute before. I couldn't take much more of this night. Finally he lifted his head and looked at me out of the corner of his eye.

"Good night, Damon," he said.

"Night," I responded, trying to sound cheerful but just sounding strained.

With that he walked outside, and the door couldn't close fast enough.

Jessica

I'd stared at the phone before, willing it to ring. But I'd never clutched it with both hands, closed my eyes, and prayed to the Pacific Bell gods. Until now.

Please let it ring, I thought. *Let it ring, and let Damon have some incredible excuse, like charity work with puppies. Please, pleeease don't let him like someone else.*

It was amazing what a few hours of phone silence could do to damage your ego. I'd pretty much already decided that Damon had spent the afternoon over at some hot girl's house having tickling matches and watching teen-romance movies. Just thinking about it made me feel like barfing.

"Jess, what are you doing?" Elizabeth asked, walking into the den and dropping into the big, comfy chair. She grabbed the remote and immediately started channel surfing. She knew I hated when anyone did that. Lucky for her I hadn't been paying a shred of attention to the TV.

"Nothing," I said, tossing aside the portable telephone and grabbing the *Mode* magazine from the coffee table. I started flipping through it absently, paying no attention to the brightly colored ads and beauty advice. My brain was still concentrating a hundred percent on the phone.

Please ring, I thought. *If you let it ring, I'll never abuse call waiting again.*

"You're waiting for Damon to call," Elizabeth said matter-of-factly, staring at the TV screen as she flipped from one channel to another.

"No," I said, which wasn't technically a lie. I was praying, not waiting.

"Whatever," Elizabeth said, finally settling on a music-video channel and laying the remote aside. "He's gonna call."

The phone rang at that second, of course. If Elizabeth said something was going to happen, it did. Even the Pacific Bell gods knew she was supposed to be right all the time.

"See?" she said.

I pounced on the phone and hit the talk button before the first ring had even ended.

"Hello?" My heart was in my throat, and I was gripping the phone so hard it almost popped out of my hand.

"Hey, Jess," Damon's voice resonated through the speaker. I loved that he could immediately tell my voice from my sister's. There aren't many people who can do that. Sometimes my *parents* can't even do that.

"Hey!" I said, sitting up straight. Now we were going to get to the bottom of this. He had to tell me where he'd been all afternoon.

"Sorry I wasn't here when you called," he said with a sigh. "I had to stay after school with Mrs. Serson." Whew! It wasn't another girl. But then what was it? Was he in trouble?

"So listen, can I speak to Elizabeth?" Damon said.

At least that was what I thought he said. There was no way I could have heard that right.

"What?" I asked.

"Is Elizabeth around?" he asked, this time sounding tired and annoyed. Wow. Not only was he in a bad mood, he hadn't given up any info as usual, and he wanted to talk to Elizabeth. This day just couldn't get any worse.

Part of me wanted to just yell at him—ask him who he thought he was, calling here and asking for my sister after I'd spent the entire afternoon not flirting with Chris Grassi and obsessing about where Damon was and whether or not he was cheating on me. How could he be so totally insensitive?

But I was too angry and confused to put my

thoughts into any kind of coherent order. Instead I just thrust the phone toward my sister without saying good-bye to Damon.

"It's for you," I said.

Elizabeth sat up and gave me a quizzical look. Then she slowly reached for the phone and brought it to her ear.

"Hello?" she said, sounding confused. I just sat there, watching her for any kind of clue as to what Damon wanted. She looked at me, shrugged, and shook her head.

"Right," she said. "Right. That sounds cool." Then she laughed.

I got up and walked out of the room. I was dying to know what they were talking about, but I had my pride. There was no way I was going to stick around and listen to my sullen, distant boyfriend joke around with my sister.

Damon

I was still writing down the definition of *irony* when the bell rang to end English class on Tuesday morning. I glanced down at my notebook and realized it was *full* of notes. Full. Any page in any of my notebooks usually started out well—date written neatly on the top-right-hand side of the page, topic written in perfect script and underlined. Then there would be a couple of lines of notes written in the same, perfect script, then a couple of lines written in a bigger, lazier way, then some doodles, and then a whole lot of blank space, which represented the span of time when I was too tired to pay attention.

This page started out the same way but continued in a semineat cursive all the way down the page. No doodles. No blank space. Just information. I almost couldn't believe it.

I slammed my notebook shut, shoved it in my backpack, and stood up with a jolt. Mrs. Serson was erasing the board at the front of the room.

"Hi, Mrs. Serson," I said, zipping up my

backpack as I walked sideways down the aisle.

"Hi, Damon," she said, smiling over her shoulder. "You were very attentive today."

I looked at the floor. "Noticed that, huh?" I said. "I guess I was just more awake than usual." I held my breath, unable to believe what I'd just said. Had I just admitted that I was usually half asleep in her class?

"Well, that's always good to hear," Mrs. Serson said with a laugh. I guess she hadn't even noticed my slip. She clapped the erasers to get rid of the dust and bent behind her desk to pick something up.

"I called Elizabeth Wakefield last night," I said, standing on my tiptoes to see what she was getting back there. No luck. "She's psyched about *Our Voices,* and she said she's going to get Anna Wang and Salvador del Valle and a couple of other people to submit stuff."

"That's wonderful!" Mrs. Serson said, coming up with a big canvas bag that was so full, she had to struggle to get it up on top of the desk. When she put it down, it immediately spilled over and a bunch of thin books fanned out across her desk. I started grabbing them up and straightening them into a pile.

"Thanks," Mrs. Serson said, wiping a strand of hair off her forehead.

"No problem." I glanced at the book in my hand. The one on top had a brown cover and the title *Echoes* spelled across the front in red block letters.

"What are these?" I asked, placing it down with the others. I wanted to flip through it, but I thought that might be rude. It was Mrs. Serson's stuff.

"They're literary magazines from other schools," she said, sitting down in her metal rolling chair. She looked at the stack like it was going to attack her. "I wanted to go through them all before our next meeting to get ideas for *Our Voices,* but I don't know if I'm going to have time." She leaned forward and propped her chin on her hand. "It seems like I always have too many papers to grade and too many journals to read. Maybe I shouldn't give you guys so much work." She raised her eyebrows at me, and I laughed. She was obviously kidding. No teacher ever thought they were overworking their students.

"Maybe I can go through some of them," I said, picking up *Echoes* again. "It's not like I have a ton of stuff to do." I never thought I'd hear myself say those words, but with things at home being taken care of by someone else, I did have a lot more free time on my hands.

She sat up a little straighter, but she still looked doubtful. "I don't know," she said, grabbing the next book and thumbing through it. "I don't want to ask you to do too much. What about your homework?"

I shrugged. Homework had actually never been a problem for me. I always did it after the girls went to bed. Now I sometimes even got to do it when it was still light out. "Why don't I just take a few?" I said, picking up about ten books. "If I get through them, I'll take a few more, but I promise I won't let it take up study time."

Mrs. Serson reached over and took half the books back. "That's enough for you," she said, eyeing what was still left in my hands. "You can have these back if you finish those, like you said."

"Okay." I put the books in my backpack. "What am I looking for?"

"Anything that looks good to you, whether it's the layout, or the theme, or the colors," Mrs. Serson said, sliding the other books to the side of her desk. "Write down anything you like. I trust your judgment."

"You do?" I said, sounding a little too childish and eager. Mrs. Serson laughed.

"Yes, I do," she said. "Don't be so surprised."

Damon

She glanced at me and then at the clock. "You should get going to your next class."

"Right." I headed out the door, but halfway there, Mrs. Serson stopped me.

"Damon," she said. "Thanks."

I turned and smiled at her. "No problem," I answered. "I'm happy to help." And I really was.

Jessica

"So, when can I see you again?" Chris asked, leaning in way too close to me.

"You mean, when are we going to meet to work on our project again?" I said, taking a step back. We were standing by my locker before lunch, and Chris was making it more and more obvious that he was *very* glad to be my science partner. The kid was shameless.

"Right, right," Chris said with a slow grin.

Just then I saw Damon walking down the hallway toward us. I stepped back even farther, my heart pounding. Damon looked at Chris's back, then at me. There was no way he wasn't going to be jealous this time. Chris couldn't have made it more clear that he liked me if he had my name tattooed across his forehead.

I watched Damon, waiting for him to come over and put his arm around me possessively, or tell Chris off, or tell *me* off. I was so nervous, my pulse was racing.

"Hey, guys," Damon said when he reached

us. That was it. He didn't touch me, and he certainly didn't threaten Chris. What was going on here? Didn't Damon *get* jealous? If I saw him talking to some popular girl this way, I'd be so green, I would need twenty gallons of makeup to cover it.

"Did you want to talk to me?" I asked Damon hopefully.

"Well, if you guys are busy, it can wait," Damon said, casting a glance at Chris. Unbelievable. Not only was he not jealous, he was willing to give up time with me and *leave* me with Raging Hormone Boy.

"We are kind of busy," Chris said.

I shot him a look of death. "No, we're not," I said, wrapping my arm around Damon's. "We can talk later," I told Chris. Then I practically pulled my catatonic boyfriend toward the lunchroom.

"So," I said, grinning up at Damon as we made our way down the crowded hallway. "Do you have something for me?"

Damon looked down at me, a confused expression on his face. I noticed a little blush creep onto his cheeks. "Um . . . no . . . did I forget something?" he asked, running his hand through his hair. "It's not, like, an anniversary or something, is it?"

My blush was a million shades darker than his. Boys could be so dense sometimes. Didn't he know I'd remind him for at least a week ahead of time if our anniversary was coming up? *"No,"* I answered. "It's lunchtime. You were supposed to bring me one of those amazing cookies."

Damon squeezed his eyes shut as we rounded the corner and pushed through the double wooden doors into the cafeteria. "I'm so sorry," he said. "I totally forgot to ask my mom to bring them home."

I tried to squelch the growing feeling of dread that had been forming in my stomach since yesterday. The dread that Damon was going to dump me any second. He'd dissed me, he wasn't jealous that one of the hottest guys in school was flirting with me, he wasn't telling me anything about his life, and now he was breaking promises. It couldn't really get much worse.

By the time we'd sat down at a table, I was so worked up, I couldn't even think about eating. Damon, however, didn't have that problem.

"So, what's up with you?" he asked, tearing into a tuna sandwich he'd brought from home as if it was a huge piece of chocolate cake he couldn't wait to savor.

"Not much," I said, sipping my water. *Not much aside from the fact that you're calling my house to talk to my sister and making her laugh while you're hardly even acknowledging that I exist.* And now all of a sudden he seemed to be in a great mood. What was the deal? And if he was going to break my heart into a million pieces, why didn't he just go ahead and get it over with already?

"What's up with you?" I asked, but my heart wasn't in it. It wasn't like he was ever going to answer me.

"Well, I'm actually working on this new literary magazine," he said, taking a gulp of his fruit juice.

I think my mouth dropped open. I wasn't sure because I was too busy staring at him like he'd just spoken in French to notice exactly what *I* was doing. "You're what?" I said, when I finally remembered how to use my voice.

"Yeah," Damon said, leaning his elbows on the table. His eyes were shining with excitement as he spoke. "Mrs. Serson is starting it up, and she asked me to be on this board of students who are helping her." He paused to take a bite out of his sandwich, which gave me enough time to process the fact that (*a*) he was sharing and (*b*) he was into *writing?* Since when?

"That's why I called Elizabeth last night," he said through a mouthful of food. "I wanted to ask her if she would contribute something."

Well, at least that cleared up *that* little moment of weirdness. But what was Damon doing getting involved with the geek sector? "Wow," I said. "That's . . . cool." It was pretty much all I could say at that moment. There was just too much random info to process. Damon had ditched me for a school meeting. He was excited about a literary magazine. My cute yet perpetually uninvolved boyfriend.

This settled it. I really didn't know him at all.

"Mrs. Serson is so cool," Damon gushed, his eyes glazing over with admiration as if he was talking about a saint or a supermodel or something. "She really likes my ideas, and she's different from other teachers, you know? She's young and friendly, like a real person. You can really talk to her and . . ."

As Damon babbled—one more thing he'd never done in all the time I'd known him—yet another dreadful sensation crept over me, but this time I knew I was right. It explained everything. It was all falling into place, but I didn't like what that meant.

Jessica

It can't be, my brain protested, but as I watched the light bounce in Damon's eyes, I knew I'd figured it all out. Damon *was* keeping something from me. And he *was* seeing someone behind my back—sort of.

Damon had a crush on Mrs. Serson.

Yuck.

Lacey

I walked out of history class on Tuesday afternoon and headed for my locker. Sure, it was all the way on the other side of school, and sure, I didn't really need to get anything from it or put anything into it, but I needed to go there because I just needed to. I started to walk a little faster and concentrated on giving all the seventh-graders I passed dirty looks. I didn't want to think about the real reason I was going entirely out of my way to go to my locker for the third time that day.

I wasn't going to think about it.

The clock that hung above my locker said I had exactly two and a half minutes to get to my next class. Plenty of time.

I raced through my combination and yanked at the lock. Of course, it didn't open because that was what happened when you raced through it. I took a deep breath, closed my eyes, opened them again, and very slowly went through the combination.

When the lock popped, I opened the locker carefully, deliberately, telling myself not to look down. If there was anything unusual there, it would catch my eye naturally. I didn't have to look for it. But nothing caught my eye. Not as I fixed my hair in my locker mirror, not as I fished through the top part of my locker looking for a book that I didn't even need.

Finally I rolled my eyes, gave up, and dropped to my knees. It took all of five seconds to go through the pile of debris at the bottom of my locker. I found an earring I'd been missing for months, a cracked CD cover, and a pack of gum, but nothing else important.

No note.

Yes, that's right. I was looking for a note from Richard. I'd been looking for a note from Richard all day, but there hadn't been one. I hadn't even seen Richard himself all day.

And as I stood there unable to move, I had to admit it to myself.

I was disappointed.

Blue
Journal Entry for Mrs. Serson's Class

Watching the crest,
I forget to paddle out.
Too wrapped up in words
And the color of your hair.

(Thought I'd keep going with the poetry
thing. Is that cool?)

Damon
Journal Entry for Mrs. Serson's Class

I feel like I'm jealous of everyone lately.

I'm jealous of Ben because he hangs out at our house all the time and everyone thinks he's so great.

I'm jealous of my sisters in a very minor way. Because they like Ben and they don't know any better. Part of me wishes I could be that young and innocent and just love everyone.

And now I'm jealous of one of the guys in my grade. His name is Chris. I figure I can say that because there are about ten Chrises in the eighth grade, so I won't really be naming names. I'm jealous because he's spending a lot of time with a girl I care about. And I feel like I can't say anything without looking like an immature idiot. And if I look like an immature idiot, this girl won't like me anymore. And she won't want to spend time with me. And I don't think I can handle that right now.

Lacey

I finally saw Richard right before lunch. He was outside the gym, leaning over the water fountain, taking a nice, long drink, and his hair was, of course, flopping perfectly over his forehead. He didn't see me, which was good because I wasn't sure I could do this. Walking up to him was going to take a lot of pride swallowing, and I wasn't sure if I could force it all down without choking.

I'd changed my mind and was going to just forget it when he looked up. Had to happen, right? He wiped his mouth with the back of his hand, looked behind him as if I might be standing there like an idiot waiting to talk to someone else, then stuck his hands in his pockets.

"What's up?" he said.

"Well," I said, opting for the coy thing, which was better than the pathetic thing. "There were no notes in my locker today." I pulled on the hem of my yellow T-shirt, put my

115

hands on my hips, and arched one eyebrow, but it felt false. Probably because the outward cool was not natural with the way my heart was pounding in every part of my body.

Richard's eyes darkened. "Some news flash," he said. Then he started to walk toward me— past me.

"Wait," I said, before I could stop myself. He was behind me now, but I heard and felt him stop. I turned around slowly with no idea at all of what I was going to say.

"Yeah?" Richard said, turning to face me. He was wearing a silver band on the middle finger of his right hand. I'd never noticed that before. I liked it.

"I wanted to say thanks," I said, staring at the ring, glad it was there to give me something to stare at. I never had this much trouble talking to anyone. It was freaking me out. "For driving me home yesterday, I mean." I sounded so wimpy and pathetic. Like Jessica Wakefield talking to her little Damon puppy dog. "And I guess, um, I'm sorry I hung up on you like that."

Richard took a step closer to me, and I waited for the inevitable clever dig followed by the ever ready smirk. "Did you . . . I mean . . . did everything . . ." He paused and cleared his throat, and that was when I finally looked at his face. His slightly pink face. Was it possible? Was Richard Too Cool Griggs feeling less than cool?

"You didn't get in trouble, did you?" he finally managed to say.

I adjusted my backpack strap and then found my hand at my throat on my necklace. I was fidgeting, but I didn't care much anymore. Not now that I knew Richard was still talking to me. And that he wasn't feeling too slick either.

"No," I said. "I got home just in time, actually." I snorted a laugh and blushed even harder. "I think my stepmonster was mad she didn't get to ground me."

I almost covered my mouth with my hand. I never called her my stepmonster in public. It sounded so juvenile. But Richard didn't even blink.

"Good," he said, scuffing at the floor with his boot. " 'Cause if you were grounded, I . . ."

My heart was in my throat. If I was grounded, he . . . what? *What?* I almost smacked myself on the head to try to clear the jumbled thoughts. What was wrong with me? Why was I so nervous and excited and incoherent?

He looked at me with his big green eyes, and I couldn't have torn myself away if I tried. This was it. I couldn't believe it, but I was actually falling for Richard Griggs. It was totally stupid. Not only was he the biggest player in school, but I hadn't even been single for twenty-four hours. I had to get a grip.

"Well, if you were grounded, I wouldn't be able to ask you out," Richard said finally, glancing away for a split second.

"You could ask—I just wouldn't be able to go," I said, finally recovering a shred of my usually incredible wit.

Richard cracked a grin, turned, and started walking toward the cafeteria. I fell into step with him. We were both looking straight ahead, and we were both grinning like idiots.

"So, Frells," he said. "Hypothetically, if I were to ask you to . . . I don't know . . . play basketball with me at the arcade . . . what would you say?"

"Hypothetically?" I said, raising my eyebrows. "Hypothetically, I'd say you're on."

"Hmmm . . . ," Richard said, holding the cafeteria door open for me and earning an impressed glance from one of the lunch ladies. I could get used to this. "So . . . how would Friday be . . . for this hypothetical date?"

"Friday would be great," I said sincerely, pushing a curl out of my face. Then I grinned and turned away. "As long as I stay ungrounded until then," I said as I walked away.

"Keep me posted!" Richard yelled after me. And I laughed. And it felt really, really good.

Jessica

"Jess, hurry up!" Bethel whined at me as I adjusted the elastic brace on my ankle and started digging through my duffel bag. "We're going to be late for practice, and I don't feel like getting screamed at today. It's just this thing I have against public humiliation."

"Just give me a sec, okay?" I said. I knew I had packed my blue shorts that morning, but I couldn't find them. I wasn't going to be any good at track practice without them. "You know, having you hanging over me and being all tense isn't making this any easier."

"Uh, Jess, what are you looking for, exactly?" she asked, glancing over my head into my locker.

"My blue UCLA shorts," I said, tossing my bag down in disgust. Bethel reached over my head and pulled my shorts out of the top part of my locker, twirling them around her finger.

"These UCLA shorts?" she asked, raising her eyebrows and trying not to laugh at me. I don't know why she bothered. She was always laughing at me. But it was kind of okay because I laughed at her when she was being idiotic too.

"All right, let's go," I said, grabbing the shorts from her. I mashed them into my bag, slammed my locker, and started off toward the gym. But as soon as we got around the corner, I stopped in my tracks. There, down the hall, walking toward the front door with their backs to us, were Damon and Mrs. Serson. My heart skipped a beat. He was carrying one of her bags, and her head was bent toward his just a little. They were obviously in the middle of a serious conversation.

The kind of conversation Damon and I pretty much never had.

"What's the matter?" Bethel said, popping the silver barrette out of her hair, rearranging everything so it looked exactly the same as it just had, and popping the barrette back in.

"Nothing," I lied. Then Damon and Mrs. Serson turned to walk out. When the door opened, the sunlight spilled in, and I could see his profile clearly. He was looking at her with all this admiration in his expression.

He never looked at me that way.

"I have to go," I said, still staring at the door

Jessica

Mrs. Serson had just disappeared through with my boyfriend.

"What?" Bethel said, throwing up her hands. "Go where?"

"Just tell Coach I'll be a little late," I said, jogging down the hallway, my bags slapping against my back.

"Whatever!" Bethel called sarcastically. I ignored her. I was angry and confused, and I was finally ready to confront Damon. I couldn't let this moment pass, or I would never get these feelings out. I just hoped I would catch Damon by his bus and not getting into Mrs. Serson's car or something. Not only would that be gross, but I was pretty sure my heart wouldn't be able to handle it.

Damon

After I helped Mrs. Serson get all those literary magazines to her car, I started back in the other direction to walk home. I was looking forward to getting there again today. Ben had a job to do this afternoon, and he was supposed to leave as soon as I got home. I could spend some time playing with Kaia and Sally and then go through some of the magazines while Sally did her homework and Kaia took her nap.

It would be just like the good old days.

A little laugh bubbled up in my chest. Two months ago I never would have believed I'd be calling those days the good old days.

"What's so funny?"

I stopped in my tracks at the sound of Jessica's voice. Jessica's *angry* voice. She walked up in front of me, carrying her backpack and her gym bag and looking all kinds of irritated.

"What's up, Jess?" I asked, clueless as to why she might be mad about anything, let alone at me.

123

"What were you and Mrs. Serson talking about?" she asked.

I blinked, totally taken off guard. A car horn honked, and we both jumped. That was when I realized we were standing in the middle of the road. I held Jessica's arm and moved her onto the sidewalk, but she shrugged me off the second we got there. This was so weird.

"What do you mean?" I said, running my hand through my hair. "We were just talking about . . . stuff."

"No!" Jessica said so loudly, a couple of people stopped to stare. Not that I cared. Jessica seemed to, though, since she lowered her voice and took a step closer to me. "I want to know specifics," she said, tucking her chin and looking up at me. "I can't take these vague answers anymore." I had no idea what she was talking about.

"C'mon, Damon, what's going on with you?" Jessica demanded, her eyes wide but kind of nervous looking. "Is something going on at home? Something you can tell Mrs. Serson about but not me?"

Was *that* what she was so upset about? I mean, maybe I didn't tell her everything, but why would she want to hear about Ben and my sisters and my mom? And . . . what if she thought I was whining and thought I was annoying and then . . . and then what if she dumped me?

"Jess," I said, rubbing my forehead with one hand. "Look, I just don't want to bore you with my problems."

She half sighed, half grunted. "Why not?" she shouted. This time she didn't even notice the stares.

"Because," I said, racking my brain for something to say that didn't sound totally stupid. I was still so surprised that she was angry and stunned over the fact that I was being ambushed that I was having trouble making a clear thought. "You don't need to hear that stuff," I said. "Besides, it's not a big deal—"

"I don't care if it's not a big deal," Jessica said. I could swear there were tears in her voice. "I'm your girlfriend. And in case you've forgotten, Mrs. Serson *isn't*. And I'm sorry, but I'm also your *friend*. I care about you. I want you to tell me about the things that are a big deal *and* about the things that aren't a big deal."

One frustrated tear spilled over onto her cheek, and it practically broke my heart. I just wanted to hug her, but her body language was telling me to stay away. Instead I fumbled for an apology. I didn't want to see her hurt, and knowing I had somehow done it killed me—even though it hadn't been on purpose.

"Jess, I don't know what to say except—"

"Try telling me one thing about your life," she spat out, raising a finger. "This is ridiculous. I mean, I've known Chris Grassi for two days, and I already know more about him than I know about you!"

At the sound of Chris's name, I felt like I had been slapped. Her being angry at me was one thing. I could handle that and try to do something about it. But how could she throw Chris Grassi's name in my face?

"Really?" I said, taking a step back. "That's great. I'm glad Chris is such a great guy."

"What?" Jessica said, her eyes squinting up.

Suddenly all I could think about was escaping.

"You know what? I have to go," I said. I tried not to let myself look at her hurt, betrayed face as I turned to go. I felt hurt and betrayed too. First my mom and now this. Obviously I'd been replaced in Jessica's life too.

By the time I got home, I was somewhere in between totally angry and really worried. I'd never done this whole relationship thing before. What if I'd totally screwed it up? If I had, I was clueless about how to fix it. But what if it wasn't even fixable? What if Jessica really did like Chris Grassi better than me? I wasn't ready to give Jessica up. I liked her. A lot. But whenever I started thinking about what I might have done wrong, I started to get angry again. She was the one bringing up other guys. It's not like I was the one working on a science project with one of the most popular kids in school. I just hadn't told her everything about my whacked-out home life. Excuse me for being a private person.

Then the little voice in my head reminded me that I hadn't been a private person lately. I'd been spilling my details to someone, just not to Jessica. And that was what she was mad about. Apparently she did want to know about my stupid problems. And maybe . . . maybe I should be grateful for that.

Needless to say, by the time I got to our front door, I was monumentally confused. I couldn't wait to spend a simple afternoon finger painting or doing something else that was equally mindless with my sisters.

I opened the door and was about to say hello when I realized the place was deathly quiet. Actually, I'd noticed it while I was still outside (usually whatever Kaia's doing is loud enough to be heard from the yard), but I was so preoccupied, I hadn't really registered it. But now I could see the trailer was totally deserted.

Great. So much for my mindless afternoon of sibling bonding. I wondered where Ben had taken them. Maybe they were at the mall, and Ben was showering them with gifts to win them over. I snorted a laugh at that obnoxious thought and shook my head. In my gut I knew Ben wasn't trying to win them over. He was just being a nice guy. I really had to chill.

Taking a deep breath, I walked over to the fridge and grabbed a juice box. I dropped it on the counter and was about to pierce it with the flimsy excuse for a straw when a note lying on the counter caught my eye.

For some reason, a chill ran straight through me.

I forgot about the juice box and picked up the note. Up until that moment I had never seen Ben's handwriting, but as I read the note, I knew I'd never forget that big scrawl for the rest of my life. The note read:

D—
   Sally fell from swing. Went to ER at Fowler Memorial. Don't worry.
                                    —B

And then I was at the bus stop. I couldn't even remember how I got there. I mean, I must have dropped the note, grabbed some money from the emergency stash, and run because I was out of breath and I had a couple of crumpled dollars in my fist, but I couldn't actually remember getting there. All I could remember was the one thought that kept repeating itself in my mind.

Please let her be all right. Please let her be all right. Please let her be all right.

Jessica

That afternoon I had the best track practice of my life. I beat my personal records in both the four-hundred-meter and the eight-hundred-meter dash. I did fifty sets of stairs (when we have to run up and down the bleachers at ridiculous speed), and I even doubled up on sit-ups. Fighting with Damon was apparently good for my stamina. But when I got home, I crashed. Hard.

When Elizabeth walked into my room to tell me Mom wanted me to empty the dishwasher, I was lying facedown on my quilt, my lips mushed to the side by the corner of a pillow. My legs and arms were flung out like a rag doll's, and they all felt like they weighed a hundred pounds each. Empty the dishwasher? I'd be lucky if I could lift one fork.

"What's wrong?" Elizabeth asked, squatting beside the bed and leaning over to catch my eye. She must have known I wasn't going to move to face her if she sat anywhere else.

"Tiiired," I said through the pillow fabric.

"Huh?"

I lifted my head about a centimeter. "Tired," I said, then flopped down again.

"All righty, then," Elizabeth said, smiling. As she stood up, the phone rang, and the pathetic girl inside my skin wanted to pounce on it. After all, it could be Damon, ready to beg for forgiveness. But I was both too wiped and too proud to do any pouncing at the moment.

"I guess I'll be getting that," Elizabeth said, reaching up and taking the phone from the night table that was inches from my face.

"Hello?" she said. I watched her for an indication of who it was. "Yeah, hold on a sec." She held out the phone to me, and my heart jumped. What was I going to say? Should I still be mad? I didn't feel mad anymore; I just felt tired. Should I act like nothing happened? Should I just let him do the talking? All of these thoughts crowded my head in two seconds, but then Elizabeth shrugged. "It's a guy, but it's not Damon."

Suddenly I felt very heavy again. It took a lot of effort to hold the phone.

"Hello?"

"Jessica? It's Chris."

"Oh. Hey," I said, closing my eyes. I could have fallen asleep right then.

"Don't sound so enthusiastic," he said with a laugh.

131

"Sorry," I said. "Long practice."

Another short laugh. "I know how that is."

"Yeah," I said. There wasn't much more I could say. I was drifting.

"So I'll make this short," Chris said.

Good, 'cause I want to pass out, I thought.

"Do you want to hang out this weekend?"

Suddenly my eyes popped open, and I sat up. Elizabeth flinched and then gave me a questioning look.

"Hang out?" I said, shooting an alarmed look at my sister. "You mean you and me . . . alone?" I knew the guy was an outrageous flirt, but I hadn't expected *this*.

Who? Elizabeth mouthed.

Chris Grassi, I mouthed back.

Oh my God, she mouthed, letting her jaw drop open as she stared.

Meanwhile Chris was talking. "Yeah, like a date," he said.

"Could you . . . hold on a second?" I said. My hand was over the mouthpiece before he'd finished saying the word *sure*.

"What do I do?" I whispered at Elizabeth. I was blushing, and I felt all flustered. It was flattering to have the hottest guy in school ask me out. However wrong it was.

"What do you mean?" Elizabeth said. "Say no . . .

132

unless you're planning on breaking up with Damon."

I didn't say anything.

"*Are* you?" Elizabeth hissed.

"No," I answered. But I was tempted to say yes to Chris. I wasn't *planning* on breaking up with Damon, but at the moment I had no idea where our little relationship was going. If it could even be called a relationship.

"Jess," Elizabeth whispered, standing up straight. "You have to talk to him." She gave me a serious look. "What do you want to do?"

I glanced down at the phone and thought about Damon. I saw his laughing eyes, his amazing smile, and felt his arm around my shoulders. I was still mad at him, and there was still the distinct possibility that he had a crush on a teacher (again, ew), but it didn't matter. I suddenly knew *exactly* what I wanted.

I lifted the phone to my ear. "Chris," I said. "I think there's been a misunderstanding."

There was silence. I didn't know Chris was capable of silence. I rushed on, wanting to fill it. "I'm with Damon Ross, and thanks for asking, but I really can't go out with you or see you outside of . . . you know . . . working on our project. . . . Okay?"

Chris sighed. "Yeah, okay," he said. "But if you change your mind . . ."

"I don't think I'll be changing my mind.

Thanks, though," I said. And then I hung up before he could say another word.. I was so nervous, I was practically shaking.

"You did the right thing," Elizabeth said firmly.

And I knew she was right.

Damon

It took forever to get to the hospital. I had all that time to imagine all kinds of scenarios. What if Sally had broken an arm? What if she had broken her head? What if she was in a coma? All from falling off the swing. I knew I had to calm down, but I was still holding my breath when the automatic doors slid open and I ran into the emergency room.

I headed straight for the front desk. But before I even made it that far, I heard Kaia yell my name. In seconds she was beside me, reaching her little pudgy arms up toward me and crying.

I picked her up and glanced in the direction she'd come from. "Shhh," I said, hugging her to my chest as I scanned the noisy, cramped room. Finally I spotted Ben—Sally was lying in his arms. As soon as I saw the bloodstained towel he was pressing against her chin, my stomach turned. "It's going to be okay," I told Kaia as I made my way to the chairs along the wall. But seeing all that blood, even *I* didn't think it was going to be okay. How did all that blood come from a little girl's chin?

"Hey," I said as I sat down next to Sally, who was also bawling. I tried to keep the worry out of my voice. "What'd you do to yourself?"

Her cries started to die down, but she didn't answer.

"She fell off the swing," Ben said. I looked at his face for the first time and noticed he was as white as a ghost. "I should have held on to the seat, but I've seen her do it on her own before."

"She swings on her own all the time," I said soothingly, finding it weird that I was comforting a grown-up. "She's the highest swinger in town."

Sally looked at me and stopped crying for a second. "She's the swinginest swinger in all the land, actually," I said, making Kaia laugh. A single tear rolled down Sally's cheek. I glanced at Ben and held Kaia out to him. We passed her over Sally's head and then I gathered Sally into my lap, towel and all.

I kissed her on the forehead and smoothed her hair back from her head as she clutched the towel to her chin. "Hey, there," I said, grinning. "What would all the other swingers say if they saw you crying? You're the queen of the swings. You've got to be brave—show 'em who's boss."

"I'm not crying," Sally said, sniffling.

"I didn't think so," I said, holding her tight. "You know, I fell off a swing once. Landed flat on my face." I looked down at her. "When I stood up, I looked like this." I stretched my mouth out, pushed my nose down with my finger, and slitted my eyes. Sally laughed, and Kaia joined in. I started to relax. If she was laughing, she was definitely going to be okay. A couple of stitches and she would be fine.

"I can't believe it," Ben said. "How did you calm them down so fast?"

I didn't know what to say to that one, so I just shrugged. But I couldn't stop grinning. I had calmed my sisters down. Ben couldn't do it, and I could. They still needed me. And that felt pretty darn good.

"Sally Ross?" a nurse said. I stood up with Sally in my arms, and we all followed the nurse toward the back room. This would all be over soon, and when it was, I was going to go home, make some food for my mom, tuck in my sisters, and call Jessica.

Suddenly I wanted to talk to her more than anything. If she'd still talk to me.

Lacey

I walked out of the pet store, relieved to leave the dry, sour smell behind me. I'd never been big on hanging out, staring at all the little birds in all their little cages as they squawked and flitted around, looking for a way out. It made me feel bad. But Kristin lived for it. She was in there right now bonding with the hamsters.

Sighing, I leaned back against the pet-store window, which was occupied by about a million gerbils. A little kid immediately nudged me out of the way. It was all I could do to keep from telling the brat off. Little kids weren't supposed to have the guts to push actual teenagers around. But I didn't say anything because that was when Richard walked out of the record store across the way.

I only had five seconds to strike an obliviously cool pose before he saw me. I think he actually caught me before my eyes were fully trained on the glass ceiling because he kind of chuckled and shook his head. Usually anyone laughing at me would push me straight into irritated-defensive mode, but it didn't happen. And that felt kind of odd—not to have the reaction I'd been having all my life. It felt kind of nice.

Richard crossed the busy mall hallway and strolled up next to me.

"What's a pretty girl like you doing in a place like this?" he asked, brushing his shoulder against mine and sending chills down one side of my body and straight up the other.

"Couldn't come up with anything better than that?" I asked, arching one eyebrow. He was trying to think of something clever to say. I could tell by the blank look on his face, but then he just laughed again.

"Forget it," he said, leaning back against the gerbil window I'd just vacated. Of course the little kid said nothing. Maybe it was a guy thing. "I've already blown my cover with you," he said, glancing at me from the corner of his eye. "So what's the point?"

I grinned. "Blown your cover, huh?" I said, rocking from my toes to my heels and back again. What was I doing? That was such eager, happy body language. Where was that coming from?

Richard looked down at my sandaled feet. "I

think you have too," he said with a smirk.

I stopped rocking and put my hands on my hips. "What?" I said, trying to stare him down. But it didn't work. He was too cute. And our covers were blown. We weren't as cool as we thought we were. At least not around each other. We both cracked up laughing.

"I won't tell if you won't," he said, turning to face me.

"I'll take it to the grave," I said in a whisper, leaning in so he could hear me. Being that close to his face caused more chills. I could get used to that feeling. I could tell from his smile and the shortness of his breath that he was feeling it too.

"Lacey?"

At the sound of my name I jumped back so fast, I almost lost my balance.

"Hey, Kristin," I said, tucking my hair behind my ear and giving Richard one seriously meaningful stare. *To the grave,* was what I was thinking. He nodded so quickly, I almost didn't see it. But I did, and I actually blushed. Blushed! I was becoming a sap faster than you could say, "Gel *who?*"

"Hi, Richard," Kristin said, looking back and forth at us as if she was trying to solve an algebra problem that was written out on our foreheads.

"Hey," Richard said. Then his friend Seth Queler came out of the record store and jogged over.

"What's up, guys?" Seth asked. His look almost mirrored Kristin's, but there was also that air of cool that guys always put on when they're around girls. Like they couldn't care less that they're around girls.

"Lacey and Richard were talking," Kristin said meaningfully. As if she knew something she didn't. I wasn't telling her anything. Not yet anyway. Right now this belonged to me. I didn't want anyone else's opinions yet.

"I wouldn't say we were *talking*," Richard said, tossing his bangs off his face and tucking one hand into his pocket. "I was just suggesting that Lacey might have an easier time with guys if she wasn't so uptight."

What? I almost started to fume, but then I realized what he was doing, and I squelched it. He was acting how he was supposed to act. How he would have acted at this time last week.

"And I was suggesting that Richard should cut down on his elaborate grooming rituals or girls might be intimidated." I looked him up and down. "No girl wants to date a guy who thinks he's prettier than she is." I paused and looked at Kristin. "I stress the word *thinks*."

Kristin stifled a giggle behind her hand, but Seth wasn't so kind.

"Oh, *man,*" he said, clapping Richard on the shoulder. "You are so burned!"

I smiled slyly. "C'mon, Kristin," I said. "There's shopping to be done." I turned on my heel and started to walk away.

"Bye, guys!" Kristin said, before trotting after me. "Lacey, you are so bad," she told me, shaking her blond curls back off her shoulders.

"He deserved it," I said, grinning. But when she wasn't looking, I glanced back over my shoulder at Richard. He looked back at the exact same time. And we both smiled.

Damon

My mom was home. The girls were tucked into bed after a dinner of ice cream and . . . more ice cream. Sally had gotten three stitches, but she was going to be fine. My mom and Ben were out in the yard, looking at the stars and talking in a low, near whisper. And I felt happy. Tired and happy. It had been some day. I had a feeling I was going to remember it forever.

It was the day Sally got hurt.

The day I stopped feeling jealous of Ben.

The day I started really being happy for my mom.

The day of my first fight with Jessica.

I grabbed the phone and plopped down on the couch. On the way back from the hospital, with Kaia asleep in my arms, I had some time to think about everything Jessica had said. And all I wanted to do now was apologize. She'd basically told me she cared about me enough to want to know everything about me, and I'd turned around and walked away. Why? Partially because I couldn't believe anyone could possibly be that interested in me. And partially because I was a big, fat baby.

I just hoped she'd forgive me. I mean, she sat there and poured her heart out and I focused on the fact that she mentioned—*mentioned*—Chris Grassi. I was the definition of jerk.

Holding the top of the phone against my forehead as if it could help me think, I tried to come up with an opening line.

"Jessica, we need to talk." No, that sounded like I wanted to break up.

"Jessica, please forgive me." Nope. A little *too* beggy and pathetic.

"Jess, I'm sorry."

That was what I really wanted to say anyway. It was simple. Straightforward. And she could either take it or leave it.

I just really hoped she took it. I lifted my hand off the hang-up button and dialed her number quickly before I could chicken out.

It rang twice, and someone picked up, sending my heart into my stomach. One of the most uncomfortable feelings ever.

"Hello?"

"Oh, hi, Liz," I said. And it was like my heart dropped all over again. The hard part still wasn't over. "It's Damon."

"Heeey," she said in this drawn-out, vague way that made it obvious she knew everything.

"Is Jessica there?" I said, gripping the phone.

"Uh, hold on a sec," Elizabeth said. There was a muffled sound as she covered the phone with her hand. I could have sworn I heard her say, "Okay . . . tell him." And then the line opened up again.

"Damon? She can't come to the phone right now," Elizabeth said.

My heart was being eaten alive by my stomach. Jessica was sitting right there next to her sister. I knew she was. And she was choosing not to talk to me.

This was so not good.

Larissa
Journal Entry for Mrs. Serson's Class

I hope you don't mind if I skip this one and I write double the amount next time! I have a huge paper to turn in, and I'm way behind!

Damon
Journal Entry for Mrs. Serson's Class

I've learned something this week. (Prepare yourself, Mrs. Serson. This is going to be a deep one!)

I've learned that change can be good. New people can come into your life and change it for the better. They don't always have to be a threat. Sometimes they might even make you see how good you have it. And make you appreciate things more. In the past couple of days I've realized that a guy I'd resented was actually good to have around. Good for my mom and my sisters, and even good for me.

But I still think that change can be bad too. I think I might lose my girlfriend. And when I think of how that would change my life . . . I don't even want to think about it. I can't let her go. And if I want to keep her, *I'm* going to have to change.

But I think I can do it. I really do.

Jessica

I'd promised myself I was going to avoid Damon at all costs. I had some serious thinking to do about what I wanted. And I knew that if I looked into those perfect blue eyes, I was going to cave in a second.

Well, I wasn't going to let that happen. I even went all the way around the back of the school so I could come at my locker from the other side, avoiding his locker in the process. But the second I came through the door, someone grabbed my arm. And of course it was Damon. And there were those eyes. He was wearing a blue shirt that made them look even more blue.

I looked at the floor. "I can't talk to you right now," I said.

"Really?" he said, tugging on my wrist until we were alone in the indented doorway of the janitor's closet. "Because I'm ready to talk. About everything."

My heart skipped a few thousand beats while I tried to find the right reply. "I brought snacks," Damon said, holding out a whole bag of chocolate-chip cookies from his mom's diner. "You know, in case all the talking takes a while and we get hungry," he added.

"You're serious?" I said, taking the bag from him.

He placed his backpack on the floor and leaned back against the wall behind him. "Want to know how serious I am?" he said. "I've got a list for you to choose from. What do you want to talk about first? Ben, the literary magazine, my dad, my mom, the hospital . . ."

"Wait, the *what?*" I said, my stomach turning. "What about a hospital?"

"I was in the emergency room for a while yesterday," he said, crossing his arms over his chest. "Is that what you want to start with?"

I reached out and grabbed his forearm. "Are you okay? Is everyone okay?" I asked, my eyes wide. I forgot about our fight and everything else, hoping his sisters and mom weren't sick or hurt. I knew how much Damon loved them, and he'd be lost if anything ever—

"You're amazing, you know that?" he said suddenly. His voice was all deep, and he put his forehead to mine, making my heart stop. "Everyone's fine. And thanks for caring so much."

I didn't know what to say, and there was a big lump in my throat, so I didn't say anything. "I'm going to tell you everything later, I swear," he said. "I'm not going to keep anything from you anymore."

"Sounds good," I said, amazed that I could even get out two syllables. People were walking by, and I know some of them were looking at us—standing there with our heads together and his arms around me, fingers laced together on the small of my back. I didn't care who was staring. All I cared about was how close I felt to Damon at that very second. And not just physically close. Close in every way.

"But right now there's something I want to do more than talk," he said. My heart was pounding, and I wanted to say something, but I couldn't think. All I could do was think about his lips coming closer to mine.

And we kissed. Right there in the janitor's-closet doorway. A real kiss. Our first real kiss.

And it was the single most amazing moment of my life.

You hate your **alarm clock.**

You hate your **clothes.**

You're going
to love
Jr. High.

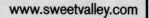

www.sweetvalley.com